JUSTICE FOR CORRIE

BADGE OF HONOR: TEXAS HEROES, BOOK 3

SUSAN STOKER

ACKNOWLEDGMENTS

Thank you to Christie M. for helping me make sure I did justice to Corrie's character. For the blind, it's not easy living in a sighted world and your suggestions helped make Corrie more "real." Thank you!

Also, thank you to Diana C. for your help with finding me a good restaurant in San Antonio. Your hometown perspective is always welcome.

And as always thanks to Rosie, Henry, and Annie for your unflagging support.

CHAPTER 1

"HELLO, Mr. Treadaway. How are you today?"

"Hi, Corrie. I'm okay."

"It's been a while since you've been in for an adjustment."

"I know, I've pushed it a bit too far."

"You've been in a lot of pain?"

"Yeah."

"Okay, go ahead and get ready. You know the drill. I'll be back in as soon as I go over your most recent X-rays with my assistant. When I come back, I'll do an exam and you can tell me where you're hurting the most. We'll do the adjustment and I'll expect you to return to see me sooner next time. All right?"

"Yes, ma'am."

Corrie could hear the humor in the older man's

voice. Jake Treadaway was in his early fifties. He had a low voice that was pleasing to her ears. He had an average build, not overly muscular, but not overweight either. He was taller than her five-nine, but not by much.

As a blind chiropractor, Corrie had to rely on her hands and her sense of touch to be able to correctly diagnose her patients and to adjust them properly. She knew there were a lot of people who still didn't believe she could do the job, but Corrie was comforted by the fact that she had a lot of clients who *did* believe in her; patients who had no issue with her disability

After graduating with her degree, she'd applied and met with the majority of chiropractors in San Antonio, and the only person who would give her a chance was Dr. Garza. He hadn't blown her off immediately upon finding out she was blind, and after she'd shown him she knew what she was doing, he'd given her a trial run. It had worked out and they were both thrilled. Dr. Garza had wanted to spend more time with his family and was happy to take on a partner. They usually alternated work days, so they could both have some time off.

There were several clients who were uncomfortable with her disability, and had refused to let her adjust them, but Dr. Garza had no problem taking on those less-than-open-minded clients.

Corrie wouldn't apologize for who she was and what she did. She'd worked hard, damn hard, to get through chiropractic college. Luckily, there'd been a few other blind students who had blazed the trail before her, forcing colleges to provide reasonable accommodations for blind students so she was able to complete the rigorous training.

Her parents had fought for her right to attend "normal" schools her entire life. She was an only child, and Chad and Shelley Madison had taught her that she was just as capable as any sighted person. She'd been born with anophthalmia, a condition where her eyes didn't form during pregnancy. She'd worn sunglasses for most of her elementary school years, but once she'd been old enough, and after a lot of begging, she'd started wearing prosthetics.

She'd painstakingly learned to clean and care for her "bionic eyes" as her best friend, Emily, called them. It had only taken one infection because of her laziness and the resulting hospital stay, for Corrie to learn it could be a life-or-death situation if she didn't properly clean and disinfect the prosthetics on a regular basis.

Corrie closed the exam door behind her and turned right to walk down the short hallway to her office. She knew exactly how many steps it was from the exam room she always used to the office, how many strides she had to take to reach her desk, and exactly where her chair would be. The cleaning service employees had learned not to move any of her things even one inch after an incident where her trash can hadn't been put back in its spot and Corrie had fallen over it one morning.

Corrie eased into her chair and thumbed through the files sitting on her desk. Their administrative assistant, Cayley, always placed the files of the clients she'd see each day in the center of her desk in the mornings. The tabs had the names of each patient written on them, but Corrie had also printed out labels of their names in Braille and placed them on the front of each folder.

Corrie reached out and grabbed her mouse, it was right where it always was, and clicked. A female voice talked Corrie through maneuvering within Mr. Treadaway's online file and medical history. She made some notes in a recorder she kept on her desk. Cayley took the device and typed up her notes on each person at the end of every day.

Finished with her preparations for Mr. Treadaway's adjustment, Corrie stood up and walked back to her office door. Her assistant, Shaun, should've been in her office by now. He would know by now that Mr. Treadaway had arrived. They always went over his radiographs so Corrie would know which vertebrae she needed to concentrate on. She'd never work on a patient without the review. She didn't want to hurt someone or, God forbid, paralyze them by adjusting the wrong place on their spine.

Shaun was about her age, thirty-two, and married with two kids. His younger child had been in a swimming accident a year and a half ago. Five-year-old Robert fell into their neighbor's pool and wasn't missed for approximately ten minutes. By the time they found him and fished him out of the water, he'd been clinically dead for eight of those minutes. The doctors had been able to revive him, but he'd never have a normal life again. The lack of oxygen had reduced the little boy to a shell of who he'd once been, and Corrie knew Shaun and his wife, Abigail, were going through financial issues trying to pay his medical bills from that time, as well as paying to keep him home with full-time medical assistance.

Corrie felt terrible for Shaun. He'd worked with her for about six months before Robert's accident, and she knew he wasn't the same man since it had happened. Lately though, his performance at work was suffering, and Corrie dreaded the talk she'd have to have with him. He'd been showing up late for work more and more often, and he seemed sullen and even borderline paranoid, always asking who was sitting out in the small waiting area and if anyone ever called for him at work.

Just as Corrie reached for the doorknob to see if she could find Shaun—he usually hung out in the makeshift break room toward the back of the clinic —she heard angry voices in the reception area, followed by a weird popping noise. She froze in her tracks and tilted her head to the side, trying to figure out what was going on.

It wasn't until she heard Cayley's scream cut short that Corrie figured out something horrible was happening.

Knowing better than to open her door and try to stop whatever was going on, Corrie stepped quickly away from the door and imagined her office layout in her head. As the popping noises and the screams continued—and got closer to her office—she frantically thought about where she could hide.

Her desk was large, and sat perpendicular to the doorway. She could walk from the door straight to the chair at her desk without having to swerve around any furniture. She kept her office purposely free of extraneous chairs and tables so she didn't have to worry about tripping over them. She could hide under the desk, but wasn't that where everyone always hid—and died doing it? If she was a crazy person hell-bent on killing everyone around her, that's the first place she'd look for stragglers who might be hiding.

The exam door down the hall was opened and Corrie heard Mr. Treadaway ask, "Who are you?" before the awful popping sound came again.

Knowing time was running out, the gunman would be at her office within moments, Corrie made the split-second decision to see if she could fit in the small area under the sink. There was no other place she could hide.

When she'd been hired, there hadn't been any extra space for her to have an office in the small clinic. A small break room had been converted for her, and the sink and cabinets still lined one wall. It would be a tight fit, an *extremely* tight fit, but Corrie didn't hesitate.

Hearing the unsteady gait of someone walking down the hall, Corrie raced over to the sink and opened the cabinet underneath. She shoved her butt in first and wiggled it around, knocking over a few odds and ends that were stored under there in the process. She drew her knees up as close to her chest as she could get them and sighed in relief as she realized she fit, barely. Her neck was bent down at an awkward angle and she couldn't breathe very well, but Corrie quickly, and quietly, closed one door, then the other, praying whoever was shooting wouldn't think to look under the sink for anyone.

At the same moment Corrie heard the soft click of the cabinet door to her hiding place engage with the small magnet that kept it shut, she heard her office door burst open.

Because Corrie was blind, her other senses had always been more acute than a sighted person's. She seemed to hear, smell, and taste what people with no disabilities couldn't. The man who'd entered her office walked straight to her desk. Corrie heard her desk chair being pulled away. Yup, he'd immediately checked under there to see if someone was hiding from him. She heard him walk to the small window and held her breath.

Corrie nearly jumped out of her skin when she heard the man's cell phone ring. He answered it and paced around her office as he spoke to whomever was on the other end.

"Yeah? Just about. No trouble whatsoever. Easiest job I've had in a long time. Haven't seen the asshole yet. Yeah, he was supposed to be here. I've got one more room to check. No, no witnesses. Yes, I'm fucking sure. He'll wish he paid what he owes us once he sees what happened to his coworkers. Fuck off. You'll hear from me when you hear from me."

Corrie breathed shallowly, trying not to make a sound. She knew she was one cough, one muscle twitch, one wrong move away from death.

The shooter sounded mean. She couldn't tell what he looked like, of course, but his voice had a unique accent. She couldn't place it, but Corrie was pretty sure if she ever heard it again, she'd recognize it. She listened as he walked around the room one more time. It sounded as if he was limping; there was a light pause between his footsteps, as if he dragged one leg a bit more than the other.

She almost had a heart attack when he came over to the sink and turned on the water above her. Corrie heard it gurgling through the pipes her knees were jammed against and even felt the pipe warm as the liquid coming out of the faucet heated up. The water turned off and she heard the killer grab a paper towel from the stack next to the sink.

As she sat under the sink, wondering if the man would somehow realize she was there and shoot her in the head, Corrie could smell the cologne he was wearing. She'd never smelled anything like it before. If she'd met a man out at a party or a club, she might find the scent attractive, but because of her circumstance, and the knowledge that she was two inches away from death, she almost gagged at the stench of him. The smell of gunpowder also clung to the man, as if he were cloaked in it. Corrie knew she'd never forget the scent of his cologne mixed with that horrible smell of gunpowder.

Finally the man limped to the end of the row of cabinets and must've thrown away the wet paper towel he'd used to dry his hands. Such a polite murderer, not leaving any trash around. She heard him open the first upper cabinet and rummage through it.

What in God's name was he doing? Shouldn't he want to get away? He'd just shot and probably killed people—was he looking for condiments now? Why wouldn't he just *leave* already?

She almost whimpered in relief when she heard the faint sound of sirens. Either someone in the clinic must've called 911 before they were killed or someone nearby heard the shots. It took the man another few beats to hear them and he'd opened another cabinet in the meantime. When he finally heard the wailing of the police sirens, he turned away from the cabinets and walked quickly to the door to the office with his uneven gait.

Corrie didn't hear the door to her office close, and listened as the man walked to the last room he hadn't checked yet. It was the small break room. Shaun obviously wasn't there, because Corrie didn't hear any more gunshots. The mystery man then walked back up the hall the way he'd arrived, and not too much later, Corrie heard nothing but silence.

The quietness rang in her ears. It wasn't normal for her workplace. Usually she heard the sounds of keyboard keys clacking as Cayley worked on her computer. She'd hear Shaun talking with Cayley, or on the phone, or with a client. Clients sometimes spoke on their phones while they waited for their appointments, or talked to each other. Hiding under the sink, Corrie couldn't even hear the hum of the air conditioner that usually drove her crazy by the end of each day. It had a high-pitched squeak that no one but her seemed able to hear.

Corrie's legs were cramping, but she was too scared to move. She couldn't see what was going on, if the man was really and truly gone, or if he had an accomplice. Maybe he was waiting to see if any witnesses, like herself, crawled out of their hidey-holes, so he could blow them away as well. She'd never been so scared in her entire life, and that was saying something.

Growing up blind hadn't been a walk in the park. She'd made it through too many terrifying situations to count, including being lost in the middle of a large shopping mall. Or the time she went out with friends in college and got separated from them when a fight broke out in the bar they were in. Corrie could hear grunting and fists hitting bodies, but had no idea which way to go to escape the danger all around her.

But this—this was a whole new kind of scary.

Corrie stayed huddled under the sink, listening as several people finally entered the clinic area. They didn't say a word, but Corrie could hear them methodically making their way through each room, saying "clear" as they entered each one. It was obviously the police, and she'd never been so glad to hear anything in her entire life.

Not wanting to get shot, she didn't dare pop open the cabinet doors to crawl out. When she heard two people enter her office, she took a chance and tentatively called out, "Don't shoot! I'm a chiropractor. I'm hiding under the sink."

"Come out with your hands up."

"Okay, I'm coming, but please, don't shoot me." Corrie's voice wobbled as she answered. She leaned against the cabinet door with her shoulder and as she expected, the small magnet holding it shut popped open easily. She tried to keep her hands in full view of whoever was in the room. She stuck them out first and swung her legs out.

"Slowly."

She nodded at the terse order. Corrie heard a shuffling sound to her right and to her left. There were at least two officers in the room. She ducked her head and emerged from the small space with a relieved sigh, staying on the ground, knowing her legs wouldn't be able to hold her up just yet anyway.

"Put your hands on your head and don't move."

She did as instructed, intertwining her fingers together on the back of her head, knowing the officers were probably jacked-up on adrenaline, and she didn't want to survive the workplace shooting only to make a wrong move and be accidently shot by the good guys. She felt her wrists being forcibly grasped and held in place. She stayed sitting, waiting for more instructions. She felt another pair of hands patting down her sides, obviously looking for a weapon. After they found nothing, Corrie felt her hands being released.

"Who are you? What's your name?"

"Corrie Madison. I'm a chiropractor here."

"Can you tell us what happened?"

"I can tell you what I know, but please...is Cayley okay? What about Mr. Treadaway? I think there were others waiting for their appointments..." Her voice drifted off as she waited for reassurance that wouldn't ever come.

"I'm sorry, Ms. Madison, they didn't make it. Now, what can you tell us? What did you see?"

Corrie turned toward the demanding voice.

Sometimes she forgot people couldn't tell she was blind. It was refreshing, usually, but she'd give anything, absolutely *anything* at this point, to be able to tell this officer that she could identify who had killed her coworkers. She tried to hold back her tears. This was no time to lose it.

"I'm blind, officer. I didn't *see* anything."

CHAPTER 2

CORRIE TRIED to follow the hostess as she led her to a table in the crowded restaurant. She tapped her cane on the ground in front of her, making sure she didn't run into any chairs or tables. People didn't necessarily take the easy way when leading her places, and Corrie had banged her shins too many times to risk not using her cane.

Besides that, Corrie wasn't at her best. She was stressed-out, jumpy, and definitely out of sorts. In the six days since the shooting, she'd experienced extreme highs and lows, and today was definitely a low.

Immediately after the massacre, she'd been brought to the police station to be questioned. She'd told the detective everything she knew about the man who'd murdered Cayley and the other innocent people. She'd told them about the shooter's cologne and how she thought he had a funny walk. Knowing her observations probably weren't very helpful, she tried to tell the detective everything she could think of anyway.

After she was allowed to leave, she'd called her best friend, Emily, and her partner, Bethany, to come get her. She'd stayed at their house that night, but refused to stay any longer than that. She was tough; she had to get back to her life.

Corrie had thought she was handling everything that had happened pretty well...at least until the funerals had started. Emily had taken her to Cayley's service and subsequent funeral, and it'd been one of the worst experiences of her life. All she'd wanted to do was mourn her friend and coworker, but the reporters wouldn't leave anyone alone. Thank God they didn't know she was the lone survivor of the actual shooting. So far, at least, the police had managed to keep her name out of the media for her safety, but Corrie knew it was only a matter of time before her name was leaked.

She hadn't slept well the first couple of nights back in her apartment, but Corrie had expected that. She kept hearing the shooter's voice in her head and she swore the smell of him was somehow stuck in her nostrils.

She thought she was finally getting back to normal, although she hadn't been able to step foot back into the clinic yet. Dr. Garza was being very patient with her. He'd hired a company to clean the small office from top to bottom and was hoping to re-open the following week. Corrie had no idea if they'd be able to make it in the same space...who would want to come and get their spine adjusted at a place where some crazy person had come in and killed a bunch of people? Dr. Garza *had* made some security changes to the front reception area. Hopefully that would make clients feel safer.

They still hadn't heard from Shaun, and it wasn't until after her initial police interview that Corrie remembered what the killer had said on his phone to somebody, that he'd been specifically looking for someone who wasn't there. It had to have been Shaun, and now no one could find him. Corrie had tried calling his wife, but the woman had been distraught because she hadn't heard from him since the massacre either.

She'd immediately called the detective who had done her initial interview and let him know what she'd remembered.

Corrie hadn't been planning on meeting with her lawyer again—she'd retained the services of one with Emily's urging—until there was more information about the case, but she'd received a threatening phone call yesterday. She remembered every word… there weren't very many to remember.

"Keep your mouth shut and you'll live."

It seemed as though her name had somehow been leaked after all.

Corrie realized the person on the phone wasn't the same man who had killed everyone in the clinic; she didn't recognize the voice. It was deep and menacing and she knew he meant every word. It pissed her off and scared her a bit at the same time.

She wasn't paying as much attention to her surroundings as she should've been as she made her way to her table in the restaurant, because she was thinking about all that had happened in the last day and trying to figure out what the hell she was going to do. She was wrenched back to her surroundings when she bounced off of someone and heard a loud crash as whatever he was carrying fell to the floor, shattering around them.

"Oh my, I'm so sorry!"

"Jesus Christ, are you fucking blind? Watch where you're walking, why don't you? How'd you like it if I came to your workplace and made you look like a schmuck in front of everyone?"

Corrie didn't like to bring attention to her disability, but this guy's words rubbed against her raw nerves. "As a matter of fact, I *am* blind," she retorted "I already apologized for running into you, but if you'd been paying attention as well, you would've seen me and you could've gone around me."

She heard the man huff and take in a breath to respond when another voice cut in suddenly. It was muted and gruff, and Corrie felt goose bumps race down her arms as he spoke.

"Everyone all right here?"

Before Corrie could pull herself together enough to respond, the busboy groused, "Hunky-dory."

"Miss? Why don't you just step over here out of the way."

Corrie gasped a bit as she felt the man who'd asked if they were okay take her elbow in his large hand and steer her off to her left. His hand was warm on her elbow. She could feel each finger wrap around her bare arm, and the feeling of safety and protection she experienced almost made her jerk away in confusion. She'd never, in her entire life, felt anything like it. She didn't understand it, and that freaked her out.

"Are you okay? You didn't get hit by any flying glass or anything?" The man's voice was soothing and calm.

"No, I think I'm all right. Thank you."

"Can I help you—"

"I'm not an invalid, no matter what you might think of blind people."

"I didn't—"

"Yes, you did, most people do." Corrie didn't know what had come over her. She usually blew off people's concerns and went on her way. She'd never, not once, been as snarky to someone who was clearly just trying to be polite and helpful as she was to this man. But after her crap week, and not liking the feeling of vulnerability that came with his touch, she was unusually gruff.

"I really just wanted to make sure you wouldn't slip on the water on the floor."

"Why? Because I can't see it? Because I'm an idiot and I'd purposely go tromping through the middle of the spilled stuff to prove a point?" Corrie breathed hard. She really wanted to stop the words that were vomiting out of her mouth, but she was so stressed, she just couldn't. She wouldn't blame the man if he turned around and left her standing there...*she* would've if their roles had been reversed.

"Well, no, because I'm trying to be a gentleman."

"A gentleman. Yeah, like there are any of those left in the world today."

Corrie felt a light touch on her hand, and heard

the humor in the man's voice as he said, "My name is Quint Axton, I'm happy to meet you."

Reacting on instinct, Corrie lifted her hand in greeting. "Corrie Madison."

"Are you meeting someone here, Corrie?" He hadn't let her hand go and Corrie was irritated with herself for noticing how large it was and how small she felt standing there with her hand in his. And she wasn't a short woman. At five feet nine, she was generally the same size, or taller, than most people, but Corrie could tell this man was a bit taller than she was. He smelled good, like soap and the coffee he'd obviously drunk sometime recently. She could hear his clothes rustling and creaking as he stood in front of her. She had no idea what in the world he was wearing that would make him creak, but she had other things to worry about right then.

"Yeah, he should be here any minute. So you can just leave the poor blind woman here against the wall and he'll be along to take care of me soon." The words came out without thought, Corrie forgetting the hostess was probably lurking nearby to guide her to her table. She just wanted this man to go. He was disturbing her on a personal level and she didn't have time to be attracted to anyone. Her life was way too up in the air right now. She mentally kicked herself for not taking Emily up on the offer to accompany her today.

"Maybe I should start us off again." The man brought the hand he was still holding up to his chest. Corrie fingered the cold metal under her fingertips, even as she was aware he hadn't completely let go of her hand. His fingers were resting on the back of it, running his thumb over the bones there as if trying to gentle her, as she tried to figure out what it was she was touching.

"My name is Officer Quint Axton with the San Antonio Police Department, and I'm pleased to meet you," he said formally.

"Oh my God," Corrie whispered, her tone of voice immediately changing to one of chagrin. She snatched her hand back after realizing what she was feeling. "Uh, yeah, sorry. I didn't mean any disrespect, I mean…"

The man laughed, and Corrie sighed in relief. The last thing she wanted to do was piss off a cop. She had enough on her plate at the moment.

"I just wanted to make sure you knew before you said something you might really regret."

"I am so sorry. I'm not usually like this. I've had a really really *really* bad week."

The officer, Quint, chuckled. "It's okay. Now, are

you *sure* you're all right here? The person you're waiting for will be here soon?"

"Yeah, he's my lawyer."

"Your lawyer?" Quint's voice dropped in concern. A concern Corrie could somehow physically feel. She ran her hands up and down her arms, trying to get warm, feeling her cane bump against her leg as it dangled from her wrist.

"Yeah," Corrie said in a soft voice. "I heard a murder. I think someone's trying to shut me up, and I have to figure out what's going to happen next."

Corrie felt herself being moved again. Quint had taken her elbow in his hand and shuffled her farther to the side.

"We're here at the booth. Do you need help scooting in?"

Corrie put her hand out and felt the back of the seat. "I've got it. Thanks."

She knew she should be freaking out right now, but she just didn't have it in her. After everything that had happened, it felt good to have a police officer take control. She had no idea if this was the table the hostess was going to lead her to or not, but at the moment, she didn't care. She couldn't help but remember the relief she'd felt when she heard the officers come into the clinic, knowing they'd be able to help her.

Corrie felt the cold plastic through her jeans and swiveled her hips until her legs were under the table. She folded her cane without thought, having done it more times in her life than she'd ever be able to count, and stuffed it into her purse at her side. Corrie moved over and heard Quint sit on the other side of the table. She didn't say anything, figuring she'd probably already said too much. It wasn't like her to blurt out her personal history to anyone, even if he *was* a police officer.

"Corrie…right?"

"Uh-huh."

"Why don't you start at the beginning."

"No."

"No?" He sounded surprised.

Corrie sighed. "Look, I'm not trying to be difficult here. But I don't know you. You could be the guy after me." She knew he wasn't, he didn't smell anything like the shooter and didn't sound like the other man on the phone, but she went with it anyway. "Anyone can go out and buy a badge and pretend to be a cop."

"Cruz!"

Corrie jerked in her seat. He wasn't talking to her, but his voice had been loud, nevertheless. He'd turned his head and barked the name in the opposite direction from where she was sitting. He'd obviously been shouting at someone across the restaurant. It wasn't fifteen seconds later when Corrie heard two sets of footsteps coming up to their table.

"Yeah, what's up?"

Quint answered the man without giving her a chance to speak. "This is Corrie Madison. She can't see, and doesn't believe I'm a cop. Would you please reassure her?" His words were not pitying, just stating the facts.

Corrie burst in without thinking. "Okay, yeah, that won't work either. If he's your friend, you guys could've planned this in advance...pick up some unsuspecting woman who will buy your story, and if she doesn't, bring in the friend to validate you are who you say you are. And the fact that I'm blind is just icing on the cake, making your entire scam that much easier."

A feminine chuckle rang out through the silence that followed her somewhat foolish statement. Corrie had forgotten there were two people who'd come up to the table. "You tell 'em. And for the record, I like you, Corrie."

"Mickie..." The voice was teasingly warning the woman to shush.

"Sorry...just pretend I'm not here...carry on," she commented, but with a hint of humor in her voice,

25

as if she was used to her boyfriend's demanding ways.

Corrie could just imagine the man standing by their table rolling his eyes. His voice was calm and reassuring when he spoke. "Yeah, you're right. We *could* be running a scam here, but we're not. The man sitting across from you *is* Quint Axton. He's six foot two, has dark hair, thirty-six years old, and has worked for the San Antonio PD for about ten years. I could tell you a lot more, but I'm trying to be brief. I'm Cruz Livingston, FBI. My girlfriend here is Mickie Kaiser. If it's not enough validation for you, I could call our other friend, Dax, who is a Texas Ranger. I understand why you're being careful, but Quint *is* who he says he is. I'd swear on Mickie's life."

Those pesky goose bumps rose on Corrie's arms again. She could tell the man was being one-hundred percent earnest. She'd gotten pretty good at reading people's voices, since she couldn't see any nonverbal cues. The fact that this man swore on the life of the woman standing next to him was about as honest as she'd ever heard from anyone before.

She held out her hand in the direction of the man standing at the side of the booth. "Corrie Madison. It's nice to meet you."

Her hand was gripped in a strong but not crushing grasp. "Nice to meet you too, Corrie." He dropped her hand and they all stayed silent for a moment. It felt awkward to Corrie, but she didn't know if it was just her or not.

She couldn't see Cruz raise his eyebrows at Quint, and she didn't see Quint motioning his friend to go back to his table with his head.

"Hopefully I'll see you around, Corrie. Trust Quint. He's one of the best officers the SAPD has. He'll do right by you."

With those words, Corrie heard Cruz and Mickie step away from the booth and head back across the restaurant.

"Okay?"

Corrie really wasn't okay. She had no idea what the hell she was doing. Would she be able to go back to work? Was the threatening phone call for real? What would her lawyer suggest? She had no idea what was going on and she felt as though her life was spinning out of control. Before she could open her mouth to spill her guts and say something wussy and out of character for her, such as "no, I'm not okay, but I think if you held me it might go a long way toward making me feel better," Corrie heard another set of footsteps approach the table.

"Ms. Kaiser? Oh! Lieutenant Axton, I didn't realize you'd be here too. This situation is a mess. I'm glad you're here."

Corrie's heart leapt in response to Mr. Herrington's words. He knew the officer by sight, so he had to be legit. She'd already pretty much believed it after Cruz's words, but it was nice for it to be validated again.

"The shit's hit the fan," Mr. Herrington continued, obviously assuming Corrie and the lieutenant were friends, and easing into the seat next to her, "and Corrie here is gonna need all the help she can get to stay one step ahead of this asshole."

CHAPTER 3

CORRIE'S HEART sank at her lawyer's comment. Lord, what now?

"Talk to me." Quint's words were terse and grumbly...that was the only way Corrie could describe them.

"Corrie? I'm assuming you're okay with him being here and hearing our conversation? I didn't realize you knew Lieutenant Axton."

"I—"

"She knows me." Quint cut off her words, and Corrie tilted her head at him, wondering what he was doing. Technically he wasn't lying, she'd just met him so she guessed that meant she knew him, but he was obviously implying that they'd known each other for a while...longer than ten minutes or so.

"This is a bit unusual. Are you here on or off the record?"

"Off."

"Corrie?" Mr. Herrington's question lay between them.

Corrie was confused. She didn't know Quint, didn't know why he was there—other than to help her not slip in the spilled water from the busboy she'd run into—didn't know why he *wanted* to be there. Had no idea why he'd said things were off the record. She trembled in confusion, wanting to have someone else help her make some scary decisions about what she was supposed to do now, but was Quint the man to help her? She honestly didn't know.

She heard the creak of Quint's clothes, realizing now it was probably the utility belt around his waist and possibly even a bulletproof vest making the creaking noises, as he leaned toward her. He put one of his warm hands over both of her cold ones. She was clenching them together in front of her. She could feel the heat from his large hand seep into her skin. When his thumb brushed back and forth over the back of her hand again, reassuring her without words, she took a deep breath and made her decision.

"Yeah, I want him here." Her decision went back

to that time long ago when she'd been lost in the mall. The first person to stop and help her had been a police officer. He'd picked her up and let her play with his badge until her parents had found her again. That memory had stuck with her throughout her life, and went a long way toward making her soften toward Quint.

Not even hesitating, Mr. Herrington started in. Corrie heard him lift his bag into his lap and rummage through it as he spoke.

"Okay, here's the thing…I got the case file from the detective and your description of the guy that came into your clinic is probably not enough to identify him definitively; it's not like you can have a smell-o-vision lineup even if they catch the guy, but that doesn't really matter. If he thinks you can identify him, you could be in danger."

"Not enough to identify him? I know I could pick him out if I heard him talk or walk, I wouldn't have to smell him."

"Right, but he could always alter those things. I hate to sound pessimistic, but a blind witness is a tricky thing and many lawyers won't take the chance on the testimony being thrown out. I'm sorry if that sounds harsh, but juries would have to one-hundred percent buy into the idea that you knew who it was without seeing him. No one wants to convict an innocent person. Reasonable doubt and all that. His lawyer would tear you apart on the stand. It'd be a hard sell."

"So…what? He gets away with it? With killing Cayley? Mr. Treadaway? All the others?" Corrie's voice rose in her agitation. "That's not fair or right. What happened to justice?" she hissed, frustrated and pissed at the same time.

It wasn't her lawyer who responded, but Quint.

"Easy, Corrie."

She took a deep breath and tried not to cry. She never cried. She hadn't asked for any of this, didn't know if she could even deal with it.

"The jerk had the nerve to call and threaten me yesterday."

"What? Did you call the cops?"

"Not yet, but it's on my agenda for today. I wanted to let you know first hoping that it would help persuade someone that I could testify."

The lawyer sighed loudly. "I don't know that it will, but it puts a different spin on your safety. I'm thinking whoever did this is scared you *will* testify and that you *can* identify the shooter. Do you have anywhere you can go until the detectives have time to dig deeper into the investigation and find more clues?"

Ignoring his question for the time being, Corrie

asked, "Are they any closer? Have they figured out who did it?"

"No. Not from what I've heard. I don't get all the up-to-the-minute information though. Lieutenant, do you know more?"

"I didn't know this was Corrie's case until today…"

Man, he's good, Corrie thought to herself. He hadn't even known *her* until today, of course he didn't know about the case.

"…but I know the detective investigating the case. We've all heard about it, of course, and been briefed on what to be on the lookout for. I'll touch base with him when I get back to the station and see what I can find out."

Corrie turned to Quint in confusion. Her head spun with all that had happened this morning.

"Okay, Corrie, do you have any more to add to what you've already told me?" her lawyer asked.

"Yeah, I think so. It might not be anything, but I thought about it last night." She paused, not wanting to throw Shaun under the proverbial bus, but knowing anything she might be able to tell her lawyer, and the police, might help catch whoever killed Cayley and the others. She felt Quint squeeze her clenched hands in support. He hadn't let go of them while they'd been talking.

"Shaun, my assistant. He wasn't there. He was *supposed* to be there helping me with the radiographs. We go over them together before I meet with the clients. Mr. Treadaway…" Her voice cracked, remembering what had happened, and she forced herself to continue. "Mr. Treadaway was waiting for me to get back in there and make his adjustments. I was upset because Shaun hadn't come to get me yet; I was on my way to see where he was when I heard the man come into the clinic."

"Have you talked to him since?" Quint asked the question this time.

Knowing he was talking about Shaun, and not about poor Mr. Treadaway, Corrie shook her head. "No, and that's really weird. We aren't buddy-buddy or anything, it's not like we phone each other on the weekends, but I called his wife and she hasn't heard from him in a couple of days either."

"Corrie, the cops know about Shaun. They've been looking for him too," Mr. Herrington told her, sounding almost impatient. "Go over with me again exactly what you overheard the shooter saying on the phone."

"He was bragging that it was an easy job and he also talked about not seeing someone and that they thought he was supposed to be there. The last thing he said when he hung up was something about whoever this guy was, he would wish he'd paid what he owed after seeing what had been done to his coworkers."

Neither man said anything for a moment after her statement. Finally, Mr. Herrington spoke out loud, obviously not asking her a question, but contemplating what she'd said. "So they were specifically looking for someone and Shaun just happened to not be there."

Quint asked, "Do you know of any reason why this Shaun person would need to borrow money?"

"Unfortunately, yes. His little boy nearly drowned a year or so ago and he's got huge medical bills. He doesn't talk about it much, but Shaun told me once he felt like a failure to his wife and his other child because they were probably going to lose the house in foreclosure since he couldn't afford to pay all the medical bills that were piling up."

Corrie turned to her lawyer. "That's what I wanted to tell you today. If they're looking for Shaun, the police need to find him before the bad guys do." Corrie supposed she should be pissed at Shaun, or at least upset at the entire situation, but at the moment she was more worried about what he'd gotten himself into. She didn't want Shaun killed on top of everyone else she'd lost.

"You need to go to the station and tell the detective this on the record, Corrie," Quint said seriously.

"Will they protect Shaun and the rest of his family? Oh my God!" Corrie suddenly thought of something she hadn't thought of before. She turned her hand over in Quint's, and looked his way earnestly. "What if they go after his wife? Or his kids?"

Quint tightened his hold on Corrie's hands. "I don't think they will. Now, I don't know who's behind this, but typically loan sharks don't go after family. They make their point with whoever owes them the money. But again, that's just typically… nothing about this case feels normal to me."

"You have to figure out what you're going to do, Corrie," Mr. Herrington told her seriously. "I'm with the lieutenant, this feels off and especially after that phone call, it's obvious that you aren't safe."

"But you just said I couldn't testify because I'm blind; that I couldn't identify the killer."

"I did say that, but I also suggested that *they* didn't know that. These aren't honor students, Corrie. If they think there's even a smidgen of a possibility you can help the police figure out who they are, and get them arrested, you're in danger."

Corrie felt her heart rate increase, but she tried to hide her trepidation. She had no idea what she was going to do, but first things first. She had to go to the police station and tell the detectives as much about Shaun as she could. Then she'd worry about what she was going to do next. She'd always been practical; her blindness forced her to be. She'd work through things one at a time. Baby steps. It was all she could do.

"Okay, if you'll call me a cab, I'll talk to them, then I'll figure out where I'll stay and I'll let you know."

Mr. Herrington put his hand on Corrie's forearm. His hand was hot and sweaty, and it felt stifling. Corrie knew the older man wanted what was best for her, but she felt suffocated, trapped inside the booth all of a sudden. She didn't know what to do and his pushing was just making it worse.

"You keep your head down and stay safe. Keep in touch with me and let me know where you'll be so I can keep you up-to-date on what's going on."

Corrie nodded quickly. "I will." She sighed in relief when he removed his arm. Surprisingly, she heard Quint shift across from her and felt him move so that his other hand came to hers. He covered her hand with both of his and squeezed, as if he knew she'd disliked the feel of her lawyer's hand on her arm. The friction and warmth of his soothing touch wiped away the clammy feel of Mr. Herrington's fingers.

"I'll take her. I have to get back anyway. My lunch hour is over."

"Great. I'd appreciate that. I have another appointment in thirty minutes. I'll be in touch." He leaned over and patted Corrie's shoulder. Corrie could hear the plastic squeak as he eased out of the booth next to her and she heard his fading footsteps over the din of the restaurant.

"You okay?" Quint asked softly, not letting go of her hand.

Corrie pulled back, knowing she couldn't get used to this man's touch, and he immediately let go. She heard him sit back in his seat. "Of course. I'm always all right. You don't have to take me to the station, you know. I can get there on my own."

"Of course you can. You're a grown woman. But it doesn't make sense for you to pay for a cab when I'm going to the same place you are."

"It just seems...I don't know...weird. I don't know you."

He ignored her statement and said instead, "I'll even let you sit in front in my squad car if you want."

Corrie laughed, as she figured he'd meant for her to. "You mean you'd actually make me get in the back where the criminals have to sit?"

"Well….it's very nice back there. A nice hard plastic bench, top-of-the-line seat restraints, and of course the nice shatterproof plastic to keep you from flying into the front seat in case of an accident or from shanking me as I'm driving."

Corrie just shook her head in exasperation. Quint was funny. She liked that. "Okay, you convinced me. Who can pass up a ride in a cop car? If I'm good, maybe you'll let me turn on the siren or something." She smiled so he'd know she was kidding. "Can you give me a moment to stop at the restroom before we go, or will that make you late?"

"It won't make me late, come on, I'll steer you in the right direction."

Corrie stood up and held out her hand so Quint could take it, loop it around his elbow and help her find her way. She was surprised when he ignored her obvious prompt and instead took her hand in his. No one had ever held her hand while leading her. She'd had men hook her hand over their arm and press themselves into her sexually, but most people were awkward and only held on to her with their fingertips, not knowing exactly how they were supposed to help her.

Quint not only took her hand in his as if they were dating or something, but he put his other hand on her upper arm as they walked through the restaurant when someone got too close and jostled them.

"Go straight about fifteen paces. It's the first door on your left. Pull it toward you to open it. Are you sure you don't need help?"

Corrie chuckled. This she could deal with. "I'm fine. I've been in enough public bathrooms to know what to do. And if I do need help, I'll ask someone who is in there." She pulled out her cane from her purse and unfolded it even as she spoke.

Quint didn't make it awkward, he simply said, "Okay, I'll be right here waiting for you. Take your time."

CHAPTER 4

CORRIE MADE her way down the hall and disappeared into the women's restroom. Quint pulled out his phone and sent a quick text to Cruz, letting him know he was headed back to the station and he'd talk to him later. He knew Cruz would ask him a million questions about Corrie and what was going on, and Quint would be happy to answer them... after *he* figured out exactly what was going on.

After reading Cruz's affirmative response, Quint put his phone back into his pocket and thought about Corrie. She intrigued him, and he wasn't usually so captivated by a woman after knowing her for such a short period of time. He'd seen a lot throughout his career as an officer with the San Antonio Police Department. People usually fit into stereotypical molds he'd formed in his mind, especially women.

Flirty, scared, victimized, angry, entitled...the list went on and on, but he couldn't for the life of him place Corrie into any of the items on that list. He'd been amused at her feisty reaction to the busboy and even her rejection of him at first was cute.

Then when he'd figured out exactly who she was and why she was at the restaurant in the first place, she'd stunned him with the matter-of-fact way she seemed to be dealing with everything that had happened to her over the last week or so. Oh, she was unsure and shaken about the phone call, but she wasn't outwardly freaking out or crying uncontrollably, and that went a long way toward raising his opinion about her.

Of course he'd heard about the shooting that had happened. All the officers had been briefed on the incident and were told to be on the lookout for anything suspicious. The detectives didn't have a lot to go on in finding the killer, and the media had been putting a lot of pressure on the chief and the department to find who had killed all those people.

Quint had even been aware there was a witness, but he'd had no idea the "witness" was blind. He still hadn't heard everything Corrie had gone through while the man was killing her friends and workers, but he would.

He realized suddenly that he wanted to know everything about Corrie. Why was she blind? Was it an accident? How had she survived? Was she seeing anyone?

His last thought brought him up short. Seeing someone? He wasn't one to have relationships with women. He wasn't a man-whore, but he'd never found anyone who he felt like he'd want to spend the rest of his life with. He'd dated women, he'd had a couple of one-night stands, he'd even thought he was in love once, but it wasn't until recently he'd decided he was missing out by being single. After watching Cruz and his other friend, Dax, find the loves of their lives, he'd seen firsthand that having someone to love, and being loved in return, could be an amazing thing.

Not only that, but he genuinely liked both Mackenzie and Mickie. They were tough women who seemed to bring out the best in both Dax and Cruz. They lightened up their gatherings and for some reason he could totally see Corrie fitting in with them. Of course he was getting ahead of himself, he'd just met the woman after all, but the thought was there nonetheless.

Quint used to think that having a serious girlfriend would be a handicap, especially for him. Being a police officer wasn't an easy job. It involved lots of long hours, including overtime, and he was in danger more often than not. Over the last year or so, there had been a lot of highly publicized cases of what the public was calling unnecessary roughness against citizens. It was tough to be a police officer today, but Quint wouldn't want to do anything else.

Quint had wanted to be a cop since he was a little kid. Most children grew out of their first dreams of occupation, but not Quint. As soon as he was old enough, he'd asked for cop toys. His mom had bought him curtains with police cars on them. His bedding was blue and white. Quint knew his parents had thought it was cute at first and that he'd grow out of it. But he'd joined the junior officer league when he was in high school and hadn't looked back. He'd gone to college and earned his Criminal Justice degree and had been hired not long after his graduation.

Quint smiled, thinking back to the green cop he'd once been. Luckily he'd started his career in the town of Bowling Green, Ohio. It was a small Midwestern college town. It was close to Toledo, but not so close that they had murders and other extreme crimes all the time. The college kids used to call it "Boring Green" because not much exciting ever happened there...other than the annual tractor-pull championships.

In time he'd needed more of a challenge, and while Quint knew his parents wanted him to stay in Ohio, he'd eventually moved south to Texas.

Quint loved San Antonio and truly felt he'd found his ideal job and police department. He had close friends and enjoyed the way the other law enforcement agencies in the city worked together. The feeling of comradery between him and Cruz, Dax, Calder, TJ, Hayden, and Conor were unique. Not to mention the group of firefighters they hung out with on a regular basis. Having so many friends who were involved with serving the city was rewarding. They worked hard, and played hard, and got along amazingly well. He knew he'd never find a better group of friends than the firefighters at Station 7 and the law enforcement officers he hung around with.

Not only that, but Quint felt a deep satisfaction in being able to find and arrest people who were a danger to society...and unfortunately there were a lot of people who were a danger to others in the southern Texas city he called home.

He'd recognized that same urge, that urge for justice, in Corrie today. She'd been disturbed to realize her testimony, because of her blindness, would be discounted. She so badly wanted justice for her friends, and wanted to be a part of that justice, he could almost feel her disappointment.

Quint hadn't been around many blind people—hell, really *any* blind people—but Corrie oozed competence and independence out of every pore. If she hadn't spoken up, and hadn't been carrying a cane, he wouldn't have known she couldn't see.

His thoughts turned to her situation. He had no idea what she planned to do after seeing the detective, but hopefully she had somewhere she could go where'd she be safe.

QUINT KEPT his eye on the door to the interrogation room. After leaving the restaurant, he'd taken Corrie to the station and released her to the care of Detective Algood. Matt was an excellent cop who'd treat her with care and make sure she was comfortable while telling him all she remembered.

He shook his head. Since when did he care if Matt treated someone with care?

Since Corrie. She'd been friendly and funny on the way to the station. He'd given her the "tour" of his cruiser when they'd first gotten in. She'd asked if she could touch the things he was explaining to her.

He'd agreed and helped her find and run her fingers over things like the switches for the lights and siren, the laptop, the shotgun safely locked in its holder. The bright smile she flashed him when he let her flick on the siren for a moment lit up her face. Even in the midst of all the shit going on in her life, she didn't hesitate to show her pleasure in something as simple as riding in a squad car for the first time.

Quint supposed it was because she couldn't see the world passing by as they drove, but she'd kept her head turned toward him, and had concentrated on him, the entire trip to the station. He'd had her complete attention as he explained proper protocol of things like when to use lights and sirens, and how he'd use the laptop as he hurried his way to a call.

They'd arrived at the station and Quint had asked Corrie to wait in the car and he'd gone around to her side and helped her out, not letting go of her hand as he walked them into the back door of the station. Her hand felt small and fragile in his, although he knew that was a lie. She was strong, if not physically, mentally. After what had happened to both Mackenzie, Dax's woman, and Mickie, Quint knew being mentally strong was sometimes a better trait to have than simple physical strength.

Luckily, Quint had some paperwork he had to catch up on, so he was able to stay at the station and finish it while Matt spoke with Corrie. He could watch and wait for her to be done and he could help her get to where she was going next. He didn't even bother to analyze *why* he wanted to be there when Corrie was finished. He wouldn't be able to sleep well without talking to her and finding out what her future plans were.

Finally, after a long two hours, the door opened and Matt and Corrie walked out. Matt looked stressed, running his hand though his hair as he looped Corrie's hand over his elbow and led her down the hall toward Quint.

Quint closed down the report he was working on, knowing he'd easily be able to finish it in the morning, and stood. He met them before they reached his desk.

"Hey, Matt. Corrie."

"Hey, Quint," Matt returned. "Thanks for bringing Corrie back in."

"You get what you need?"

"Maybe. It's more than we had to start with. I'm going to see what more we can do to find Shaun. We'd already been looking for him, but knowing he was most likely the reason that guy was there puts things in a different perspective. I have a feeling he can shed a lot of light on this case."

Quint looked at Corrie. He'd thought she was

good when she and Matt walked toward his desk, but up close, he could now see the furrows in her brow and the pinched look around her lips.

"You okay, Corrie?"

She nodded, but didn't say anything.

Quint looked at Matt and raised his chin, asking what was up.

Matt just gazed back at him with a frustrated look on his face and shrugged his shoulders. Quint shook his head at his friend.

"What? I know you guys are talking with that nonverbal man-speak crap. I'm standing right here. It's rude. I *hate* when people do that." Corrie's voice was a mixture of pissed off and sad at the same time.

Quint immediately felt bad. "Sorry, Corrie. Really. I'm worried about you. I was simply trying to ask my buddy here what was up."

"You could've asked me directly." Corrie dropped Matt's elbow and put her arms around her stomach defensively. Her stance made her look uncomfortable and vulnerable.

"You're right. I should've. I'm sorry. Come on, let's go sit over here." Quint didn't bother trying to defend himself. Corrie was right. It *was* rude. He hadn't thought so at the time but looking at it from her perspective, he knew he had to change his thinking.

There were a lot of ways he had to change his thinking, he suddenly realized. Just because Corrie was blind didn't mean she was helpless or clueless. Trying to talk about her, in front of her, when she couldn't see, was like talking about someone who didn't speak English in front of them...they'd know you were talking about them but wouldn't be able to understand what you were saying.

Quint took Corrie's hand again and led her into a small room. "There's a chair to your left." He dropped her right hand and took her left in his and guided it to the arm of the chair. "There's a desk in front of you and I'm going to go and close the door. It's private in here, no one can overhear us."

Corrie nodded and eased herself into the chair. Once she got her bearings, she didn't fumble or fidget, she just sat and waited for him to return.

Quint closed the door and pulled a seat over so he could sit next to Corrie, and not behind the desk. He didn't want to be that far away from her.

"So...what's up? Are you okay? What did Matt have to say?"

Corrie couldn't stay mad at Quint. She'd been furious when she'd realized he and Matt were "talking" right there in front of her. She'd called him on it and he'd immediately apologized. Most people, when she confronted them on the same thing, tried to make excuses or lied and said they weren't talking about her right in front of her face. Quint got points for that.

"I'm fine. I told Detective Algood about the threatening phone call. We went over everything that happened that day ad nauseam and here I am. He's going to see if he can find Shaun and figure out what in tarnation is going on."

"What about the threat you received?"

"What about it?"

Quint clenched his teeth. He'd never met such a stubborn woman before. This was almost as bad as interrogating someone. "What is he doing about that?"

Corrie shrugged. "There's not much he *can* do about it. He's going to tap my phone; if the guy calls back, it'll be recorded and we'll go from there."

"Where are you staying then?"

Corrie squirmed uncomfortably in her chair for the first time. The detective had asked the same thing and she'd tried to explain. She'd known he hadn't liked it, and Corrie knew in her gut, Quint wouldn't either.

"Home. I'm staying at my apartment."

"Corrie—"

"Really, Quint, it's fine. Look, I'm sure once whoever it is finds out I'm not allowed to testify, they'll be appeased. I'll make sure to lock my door, and I'd already decided to call a security company to install some sort of alarm."

"Can't you go somewhere to stay?"

"Like where?"

"I don't know…a friend's house? Your parents'?"

"If you were me, would you go to your friend's or parents' house if you thought for a second it might put them in danger?" Knowing the answer, Corrie continued. "No, you freaking wouldn't. My best friend, Emily, and her partner, Bethany, have a little boy. There's no way in heck I'd put either of them in danger, and I'd rather die myself than bring a killer to their doorstep who might possibly hurt Ethan. He's only six months old, for goodness sake. He can't protect himself."

Corrie was working herself into a full tizzy, and couldn't see the tender look on Quint's face.

"And my parents? Are you crazy? After all they've done for me…after they helped make me independent, you think I'd go running back and ask to hide behind them? No freaking way. I'm fine. Detective Algood is going to figure this out, and everything will go back to normal."

Corrie was startled out of her angsty ramblings when Quint put his hand on her cheek and turned her head toward him.

"I don't like it." His tone didn't match the words. He sounded amused.

"What's so funny?" Corrie asked, exasperated.

"Not what you think, obviously."

"Darn it, Quint."

"I was just sitting here thinking how endearing you are."

"What?"

"Yeah, you worked yourself up into a frenzy, but not once did you slip and swear."

Startled at his words, Corrie could only mumble, "Huh?"

"I swear all the time. I know I shouldn't, but I can't help it. Must be the company I keep. I hope that's not going to bother you." Quint knew the words coming out of his mouth were some sort of commitment to this woman he'd just met, but he wasn't sorry. "I know finding you funny is inappropriate as hell, because the reason you're saying what you said is anything but humorous, but I thought it was cute and hilarious at the same time."

Quint's tone changed with his next words. He got serious and all humor was gone. "But that's not to say I like your plan. I don't. Not one bit." He gently squeezed Corrie's hand when she opened her mouth to speak.

"That being said—I get it. I do. I wouldn't want to

put my parents at risk either. And you certainly shouldn't put Emily, Bethany, or Ethan in danger. Have you told your friend what's going on?"

Corrie shook her head. Oh, Emily knew about the shooting and what had happened of course, she'd stayed at her house right after it happened, but Corrie hadn't told her about the phone call yet.

"She's going to insist you stay with her."

"I know, but I'm going to insist I don't in return."

Quint sighed. He didn't like it. He *really* didn't like it. But what could he do? They weren't dating; he'd just met this woman today. He didn't have any say in what she did in her life. None. And he found himself hating that.

"Do you have a cell?"

Corrie looked at him as if he had two heads. "Uh, yeah. Everyone has a cell."

Quint chuckled again. Damn, she was so fucking cute. "I wasn't sure."

"Oh, because I can't see?"

"Yeah."

"Look, Mr. Cop. I'm going easy on you because I don't think you're trying to be discriminatory or a jerk about this. I'm normal. I'm as normal as you. I cook, I clean, I talk on the phone, I even use a computer. I can read, I can tell time, I can pay for my own stuff with real money, I dress myself every morning and manage to color coordinate my clothes with the help of Braille labels. I can play specialized board games and figure out what socks go with which, except if the dryer monster eats them like it always seems to somehow. I'm just like you, Quint. I eat the same, brush my teeth the same, make love the same, orgasm the same, cry, smile, and get pissed... just like you."

"Will you go to dinner with me later this week?"

"What?" Corrie shook her head. Had she heard him right? She'd just gotten done haranguing him, and he was asking her out?

"Will you go to dinner with me?" When Corrie didn't immediately answer, he added, "Please?"

"I don't know..."

"I've been attracted to you since I saw you from across the restaurant today. I don't like doormats, so when you stood up for yourself with that guy who ran into you, I was impressed. I'm even more impressed now. You don't take crap from me, you'll protect your friends with everything you have, and you have a slight sarcastic streak. You're beautiful, you're a perfect height for me, you call me out on my idiotic bullshit, even when I say it out of a lack of knowledge and not malicious intent. Call me a masochist, but I like the fact you can stand up for yourself with me. You're not afraid of me, and that's very refreshing, you have no idea. I want to take you out and get to know more about you. I want to know about all the idiots who you put in their place for acting stupid. I want to know how you can do all those things you just threw in my face. I like you, Corrie. Please let me take you out."

"Oh. After that passionate speech, I'd be a horrible person if I refused." Corrie couldn't think of anything else to say after all that.

Quint smiled, for once glad she couldn't see his amusement. God, she was so refreshing. She didn't play games, and he'd never been so attracted to anyone before. "Give me your phone."

Corrie reached down and grabbed her purse that she'd placed next to the chair when she'd sat and plucked her cell out of the side pocket she always put it in. She held her thumb to the button at the bottom for a few beats to unlock it, then handed it over to Quint.

He didn't say a word, but Corrie could hear him clicking some buttons on her phone.

"I'm assuming you use the voice feature on here to call people?"

"Uh-huh."

"Okay, I put myself in as simply 'Quint' to make it easy when you want to call me."

Feeling a bit of her inner snarkiness coming

back, Corrie quipped, "I'm going to want to call you?"

She could hear the laughter in Quint's voice when he responded. "I sure as shit hope so."

He fiddled a bit more with the phone and she heard his own cell vibrate in the room. "I hope you don't mind, but I called my cell so I'd have your number too. I'll program it in later. Here ya go, your phone."

Corrie held out her hand and Quint put it into her palm. He brought his other hand under hers and clasped her hand with both of his. "I'm worried about you, Corrie."

She inhaled. She hadn't been sure if he was going to let it drop or not. Apparently he wasn't. But it'd been so long since anyone had worried about her, Corrie had almost forgotten what it felt like. She hadn't lied; her parents had brought her up to be self-sufficient and they hadn't coddled her at all. Oh, they loved her fiercely, but they wanted her to be independent and able to live on her own. They'd done the best they could for her, and Corrie was thankful as all get out. She wouldn't be where she was today if her parents hadn't been so awesome.

Corrie knew Emily worried about her as well, but it was somehow different, especially since Bethany had given birth to their son. They had someone else to worry about now. Their first concern was Ethan, and should always be Ethan.

"I'll be okay."

Quint hadn't let go of her hand. "You'll call if something doesn't seem right?"

"Call *you*? No. I'll call 9-1-1."

"Okay, I'll give you that, but you'll call me if you're uneasy, or if you just need someone to talk to?"

"I don't know you, Quint. Why would I call you?"

"I don't really know you either, but I'm trying to. I can't help this worry that's sitting in the pit of my stomach when it comes to you and this situation. I think about you unable to see, sitting in your apartment, and someone breaking in."

Corrie started getting mad again and tried to tug her hand out of his grasp. "I told you, I'm not helpless."

"I *know* that, Jesus. I *do*. But I can't turn this off. My gut is screaming at me that there's more to this than what we've been able to figure out as of yet. I wouldn't like it if you were a man who was six foot five and a bodybuilder. I'd like to say it has nothing to do with your eyesight, but we'd both know I'd be lying. Corrie, I've been a cop for a long time. I've learned to listen to my gut. If I honestly didn't think you could take care of yourself, I'd insist on you going to a motel, or to someone's house, anyone's place other than your own. But I can see how self-sufficient you are. That competency practically oozes out of your pores. But that niggling feeling is still there. So please, for the love of God, call me if something seems off. I can check it out without embarrassing you. Then if it's nothing, you haven't felt like you've bothered anyone else. Yeah?"

Corrie ran his words over and over in her head. He was right. This was a messed-up situation, and she didn't like it either. He'd said he was worried about her. It felt good. And she liked him. He wanted to take her on a date. Why the heck was she fighting him about this?

"Okay."

"Just okay? No other commentary?"

"I don't think so."

"Thank Christ."

She giggled a bit at his response. Quint finally let go of her hand and she turned and put her cell back into the small pocket in her purse.

"Come on, I'm off duty. I'll take you home."

Corrie fought the automatic refusal that almost came out of her mouth. She was independent, yes, but it was stupid to refuse a ride. Why shouldn't she let Quint take her home? She wouldn't have to call Emily to come pick her up now or take a taxi. She usually didn't mind using cabs to get around, but with everything that had happened she knew she'd feel safer with him. Besides, she told herself, he'd need to know where she lived if she was going to go on a date with him.

"Okay, I'd appreciate that." She stood up and held out her hand, smiling at the now familiar feel of Quint's big hand wrapping around her own. It really was amazing that after thirty-two years, she'd never felt so normal when she was being helped around as she did with Quint. The simple act of taking her hand rather than letting her grab on to his elbow, even though he had no idea he was doing it "wrong," made her feel as though she was on an actual date, rather than feeling helpless. She liked it. A lot.

CHAPTER 5

DING

The loud noise from her phone made Corrie jump what seemed like ten feet. She reached over and pushed the button on her alarm clock to see what time it was. The mechanical voice announced that it was eleven forty-three.

She hadn't been sleeping well the past few nights because of everything that had happened and every little sound now made her jump. She was hyper-aware and hated it. Even the normal sounds of her apartment now frightened her. The ice maker in the refrigerator making ice, the sound of the air conditioning turning on and off, even the sound of the automated voice of her clock made her jump. Every sound made her wonder if someone was in the apartment. She'd conditioned herself over the years to almost not even hear the sounds, but not now. Corrie despised it.

She pushed a button on the phone and heard the computerized voice read the text that had woken her up moments ago.

Quint- Hey. Just wanted to check in. Just got off shift. I hate the new-and-improved shifts the chief is trying out...the hours are constantly changing. Anyway...everything ok with you?

It was a little annoying that the program read the name of the person sending the text every single time, but Corrie hadn't had a chance to get the upgrade yet. Quint had been texting her intermittently since he'd dropped her off earlier in the week. He'd come up to her apartment and checked it out for her, declaring it "bad-guy free." She'd laughed at the time, but occasionally wished over the last few days that he'd been there to check it out for her again and simply to keep her company.

She clicked on a button and spoke into the phone, knowing the program would turn her words into a text automatically. All she had to say was send after she was done speaking, and her text would go through.

I'm ok. Your shift go ok?

Quint- Typical. Seriously, you all right?

As all right as I can be. Nights are the worst. I swear

every time an ice cube falls in the fridge, it scares me to death.

Quint didn't respond for a few minutes and Corrie sat up in bed nervously. Shoot. She knew she should've kept her mouth shut. She'd always kept their conversations light and easy in the past, not even wanting to admit to herself that she was frightened, let alone Quint. She had no idea why she'd decided to let him know how she really felt tonight.

The ding of the incoming text scared Corrie again. Crap.

Quint- I have a confession.

Okay.

Quint- I've been driving past your place after my shifts this week to make sure everything looked okay.

And?

Quint- That's it.

That's your confession? Corrie didn't see what the issue was.

Quint- Yeah.

Okay.

Quint- Okay? You don't have an issue with me driving by?

No. Why would I? You're a police officer, you have a gun, you're obviously a lot more equipped to deal with bad guys than I am.

Quint- True. Now I have another confession.

Corrie smiled now. She forgot all about how she'd been scared and concentrated on the pleasure coursing through her that Quint had wanted to check on her.

Another? You like to put on women's underwear at night and prance around your house?

Quint- Good Lord, woman. No! Jeez.

Corrie giggled, waiting for him to tell her his next confession.

Quint- I'm outside your apartment now. I didn't want to text and drive so I pulled over to check on you. Would you feel better if I came up to make sure there's nothing to be afraid of in your apartment?

Corrie struggled to get her thoughts in order. On one hand, she loved that Quint had been thinking about her and wanted to make sure she was safe. But on the other hand, she didn't want to rely on him. He wouldn't always be around. She knew being in a relationship with her wasn't easy. She'd had several boyfriends and even one who had moved in for a while. But he hadn't been able to deal with her "quirks," as he'd called them.

Living with someone who couldn't see could be tough. The furniture couldn't be moved, everything had its place. There were assistive technologies throughout her house, helping her function on her own. Almost everything could "talk" and her last serious boyfriend even complained about her knowledge of Braille, wondering out loud what she was typing and saying about him that he couldn't understand.

Even after a week, Corrie knew letting Quint into her life could be dangerous to her heart. He seemed like the kind of man who went all in whatever it was he was doing. If he went "all in" with her then decided she wasn't worth the effort, it'd hurt. Bad.

She knew he was still waiting for her response. She thought long and hard. Was it creepy he was there or not? Corrie thought about it...and decided it was a bit weird, but Quint *was* a cop. He'd told her time and time again he didn't like it that she was staying in her apartment alone, so she decided that he wasn't being stalkerish, he was being protective. She spoke into her phone and waited.

I'd like that. Thank you.

Quint- I'll be up in a few minutes. I'll knock twice, pause, then twice more, so you'll know it's me.

Okay. I'll be waiting.

Corrie put the phone down on her nightstand where she was always careful to place it. Emily had bought her one of those things that were usually used to hold remote controls for the television to put her cell in each night. She'd "lost" her phone too many times in the past by putting it down in random places. She'd learned to always put it in exactly the same place so she could find it when she needed it.

She reached for her comfy terry-cloth robe that was over the back of the easy chair in the corner of her room and pulled it around her, making sure to tie it closed tightly. She wasn't wearing anything sexy, a long-sleeved sleep shirt and a pair of sleep shorts, but it seemed prudent to cover up. Corrie ran her hands over her hair, trying to decide if she should go and get a scrunchie and put it up, but finally decided against it. She combed it with her fingers and shrugged. Oh well. It would have to do.

Corrie padded down the hall to the living room and went straight to her front door to wait. She didn't wait long. She heard two knocks, then two more.

"Quint?" she asked through the closed door.

"Yeah."

Corrie keyed in the security code on the panel next to the door, then twisted the bolt and unlocked the doorknob before opening the door a crack, keeping the security chain in place.

She once again asked tentatively, "Quint?"

"Yeah, it's me."

"Okay, hang on." Corrie closed the door and undid the security chain, then opened the door fully.

She stepped back and Quint came into her apartment, shutting the door behind him. Corrie took a deep breath. He smelled wonderful. She could tell he was still in his uniform because she could once again hear the telltale creaking of the leather belt around his waist. He smelled like leather and teakwood cologne of some sort. She could also smell a slight odor of sweat. Whatever he'd been doing tonight had obviously made him perspire at some point.

She startled a bit when she felt Quint's hand at her shoulder.

"You look exhausted. You're really not sleeping well, are you?"

Corrie shrugged, careful not to shrug off the comforting hand at her shoulder. "I'll sleep when I'm dead," she quipped, expecting Quint to laugh. He didn't.

"That's not funny. I'm being serious."

Corrie sighed and turned to walk into her living room, only cringing a little inside at losing his touch. "I'll be fine, Quint. You're right, I'm not sleeping that well right now, but this will pass eventually. I heard from Detective Algood today and he said they're getting closer to finding Shaun. Once they do, he'll tell them what they need to know to catch this guy and I'll go back to sleeping a full seven hours a night. I'd love it if you could look around and make sure all is safe and secure. Then I'll be able to sleep better, I'm sure. I'll just sit over here on the couch while you look around…okay?"

Quint looked at Corrie's retreating back. He was frustrated. He hated that she wasn't sleeping at night, but there wasn't much he could do about it. He had no idea what it was about her that made him feel so much, but it was something. Something that he couldn't walk away from.

He forced himself to tear his eyes off of Corrie and look around. Quint had been in her apartment once before, the first time he'd taken her home, and just as he'd been then, he was amazed at how neat everything was. Some people might say her apartment looked institutional, it was so pristine, but when he looked closer, he could see her little touches everywhere.

There were no pictures on the walls, nor were there any bookshelves. She wouldn't have any reason to have either of those things around since she couldn't see them. There was a large television set up against one wall. She had a remote control holder thing on her coffee table and the remotes were lined up precisely from tallest to shortest within it. She was sitting on a comfortable-looking leather couch and there was a big easy chair sitting at a right angle next to the sofa. A coffee table was sitting on a tan rug in front of the couch.

He turned his attention to the kitchen and noticed there were no papers lying around on the counter but there was a stack of mail sitting in a basket.

Quint strolled over to it and looked in. It seemed as if there was several days' worth of mail in the basket. "How do you read your mail?" The question came out without him thinking. Quint winced, hoping it wasn't insensitive.

"Emily comes over once a week and goes through it for me."

Her answer was congenial enough. Appeared as if she didn't take offense to his question.

As if she had mind-reading abilities, she said, "Quint, you can ask whatever you want. Despite evidence to the contrary, I'm usually hard to offend, especially when it comes to someone asking genuine questions about assistive technologies."

"Thank you, I will. I find everything about you fascinating." Quint noticed she didn't turn his way, but thought he saw a sheen of red bloom over her cheeks. He continued checking her place out. The kitchen appliances seemed normal at first glance, but he didn't know much about what appliances in a blind person's kitchen would look like. Like most men, he lived on microwave meals and whatever he could make on the stovetop and in the crockpot. Of course, he could also grill a mean steak.

Quint looked around the rest of the living room and kitchen, and seeing nothing out of place, went down the hall to the bedrooms. He opened the first door he came to, remembering from the last time it was the linen closet. The sheets and towels were stacked neatly, and impressively, the towels were stacked by color and the sheets were all in sets. He closed the door and went into the guestroom.

The area reminded him of a hotel room. There was a double-size bed with a black dresser against the opposite wall. There was a small window with forest-green curtains and not much else in the room. Again, there were no pictures on the walls or any extra decorations. Quint briefly lifted the comforter and looked under the bed. Nothing but a few dust bunnies. Neat as a pin.

He then went into the small guest bathroom. The shower curtain on the single shower was pulled back, showing a completely empty stall. The single sink and toilet were off-white and the entire place smelled fresh, as if it'd recently been cleaned.

Quint then continued into the master bedroom. This room, at least, looked a bit more lived in. Corrie's bed covers were mussed and he could tell how she'd thrown back the quilt as she'd gotten out of bed. Her cell phone was on a little table next to the queen-size bed in another remote control holder. There was a comfortable-looking easy chair in the corner of the room and a four-drawer dresser next to the chair. The window was large and had dark blue curtains, which were tied back. He looked under the bed, and again saw that it was empty and clean, not even a dust bunny to be seen this time.

He peeked into her bathroom and smiled. It was definitely a woman's bathroom. There were two sinks and a row of lotions lined up next to one of them. There was even a tray filled with makeup in the bathroom as well. He hadn't thought about it before, but now that he saw Corrie's personal space, he realized that she'd always been wearing a bit of makeup when he'd seen her before tonight. She'd somehow learned how to apply it...and it looked good on her.

Quint took the time to glance into the shower and, seeing it empty, headed back down the hall to Corrie.

"All clear?" she asked as he came back into the room.

"All clear," Quint confirmed as he sat on the other end of the sofa. When she smiled, he asked what she was thinking about.

"Every time you move, I can hear all your equipment moving and creaking. I think I'd know in a heartbeat if I was in the same room as another cop based on the sounds of your stuff as you move around."

Her words brought home to Quint just how observant Corrie really was. It fascinated him. "What else?"

"What do you mean, 'What else'?"

"What else can you tell about me from listening?"

"Is this a test?"

"No. I'm just curious. No, that's not exactly right. It amazes me. *You* amaze me. I'm in awe of you, Corrie."

Her cheeks pinked and she bit her lip, thinking about his question as if no one had ever taken the time to get to know her in this way before. Finally she answered. "Let's see…I can smell your shampoo, at least I think it's your shampoo. It's faint, but it smells like teakwood?"

"You're good. Go on."

"And you've eaten a peppermint recently."

"Yup, right before I came up."

Corrie nodded as if she'd known she was right all along. "And I can tell you've been sweating. It's not bad, but you must've done something tonight that made you exert some energy."

Quint scooted over to sit closer to Corrie and took hold of the edge of her robe which was lying on the cushion next to him. "Had a drunk man resist arrest. I had to subdue him." Quint said the words easily, but he was blown away by Corrie. Seriously, she was fucking amazing.

"I'm sorry my apartment isn't very fancy."

"What?" Quint hadn't been paying attention really. He'd been watching his fingers play with the edge of her comfortable-looking robe.

"My apartment. I don't have any knick-knacks or anything around. There's no point."

"It's fine, Corrie. Why would you have that crap around when you couldn't see it?"

"Emily tells me all the time that she's willing to help me spruce it up. Even if I can't see the stuff, apparently she thinks it'd make me look more approachable or less boring or something."

Quint felt his teeth clenching. "You aren't boring, not at all. And you're very approachable, Corrie. You're so approachable it's taking all I have to behave myself here."

She turned her head in his direction. Quint had to remind himself, again, that she couldn't see him. It sometimes seemed as if she looked straight into his soul. Her robe was gaping a bit at her chest and he could see her pink sleep shirt underneath. It was cotton, but for some reason, on her, it was very tantalizing. It wasn't cut so low that he could see any cleavage, but he *could* see that her nipples were hard and pointed under her nightclothes.

"Oh." The word was breathy and unsure.

"Come on, sweetheart. You need to get back to bed. You're exhausted, I'm tired, it's been a long day. Come lock the door behind me and set the alarm after I go." Quint knew if he didn't get out of her apartment, he'd do something he might regret. He felt as if he was seventeen again, getting hard at the sight of her erect nipples. It was definitely time to go.

They walked to her front door and Quint opened it, but turned around to face Corrie. She looked up at him expectantly. It even looked as though she was holding her breath.

"Corrie—"

"Are you going to kiss me? I'm only asking because I can't see any nonverbal cues you might be giving off, and honestly, I'd hate to miss it, or to have you misinterpret my actions if I didn't reciprocate because I can't see you."

Quint smiled. She was so fucking cute. He loved that she was brave enough to ask, even if she flushed as she did. "No." He ran his finger over the frown lines on her forehead. "I want to wait until I drop you off at your door after our date. It's not that I don't want to right now, but I want to kiss you as your date, not as the police officer who came to check on you."

"But you're the same person," Corrie protested, lifting a hand to lightly rest it on his chest.

Quint couldn't feel her touch because of the protective vest he wore under his shirt, but he imagined what her fingers would feel like on him and it almost broke his resolve...almost. He closed his eyes for a moment, relieved that she somehow seemed to see him, the real him, even with everything she'd been through.

"I'm glad you think so, sweetheart. Now, close and lock this behind me. I'll see you in two days. Yeah?"

Corrie nodded. "Yeah."

Quint leaned forward and kissed Corrie's forehead, then drew back far enough for her hand to fall from his chest. "Goodnight, Corrie. Talk to you soon."

"Night, Quint. Thank you for checking things out for me."

Quint stood at her door, waiting until he heard the click of the deadbolt and the slide of the metal chain engaging. He hoped she'd be able to get some sleep tonight. By the looks of her, she needed it.

He practically flew down the stairs and back out to his cruiser. He couldn't believe how excited he was for his date with her. It was almost pathetic.

His phone made a noise, notifying him of a text as he unlocked his car and got in. He looked down at his phone and smiled at the text from Corrie.

Just so you know, I want to kiss both the police officer and my date. Make it happen, would ya?

Quint smiled as he typed in his response.

Count on it. See you soon. I'll text with the details.

Quint looked around as he drove out of the parking lot, not seeing anything out of place.

A MAN SMOKING a cigarette observed as the cop car left the parking lot. He then looked up to the apartment on the second floor that he'd been watching for the last week. The time was coming to give another warning. If she wanted to ignore the first two…so be it.

CHAPTER 6

"ARE YOU SURE I LOOK OKAY?" Corrie asked Emily for what seemed like the hundredth time.

"*Yes*! You look awesome!" Emily responded enthusiastically.

Corrie ran her hands down her thighs and tried to stop worrying but it was impossible. She'd asked Emily to come over and help her get ready. For the first time in a long time, she wanted to look as nice as possible for a date. It was kinda stupid because Quint had already seen her "normal" self, but she wanted to primp for him…wanted him to know this was important to her.

Emily had helped pick her outfit. Corrie was wearing jeans…of course; she rarely wore anything else outside of work. She'd paired it with a pink sleeveless top. Emily had done her makeup for her, as Corrie could only really manage blush, mascara, and lipstick. She could feel when the mascara wand touched her eyelashes and lipstick was easy enough. For blush, she used a brush and counted swirls to avoid using too much, but she never wanted to mess with foundation because it could be a disaster since she couldn't see how much was too much.

She was wearing a pair of gold hoops in her ears and a charm bracelet with some of the charms Emily had given her over the years. Corrie knew it'd make her feel better to have something her best friend had given her when she got nervous.

The outfit was topped off with a pair of cute cowboy boots. Corrie thought they probably looked silly and was going to wear some sandals, but Emily convinced her they looked great.

"Why am I so nervous, Em?"

"Because you like him."

"I do, but…"

"Cor, you *like* him. From what you've told me this week, he's been great. He's been over here and seen how bare it is…relax. He's into you. Just go with it."

"What if I knock over my glass? Or drop food in my lap or—"

"Jesus, Corrie. Get over it. He knows about you. I think he'll be cool. Take a deep breath."

"You're right. Did you feel this way when you went out with Bethany for the first time?"

"No. I actually thought she was a bitch. You know this story…we met at that Gay Pride event in Austin and her girlfriend at the time badmouthed me. I thought Bethany agreed with her and I was pissed. But later, she met back up with me and told me she had no idea her girlfriend was such a bitch, and she'd dumped her. We spent the rest of the weekend hanging out together and realized we had sparks. The rest is history."

Corrie hugged her friend. "I'm so happy for you guys. Seriously, Bethany and you make a great couple. I know you were worried that you're ten years older than her, but I'm glad you both got over that. You're perfect for each other."

Emily hugged her back. "I know, you tell me practically every time you see me."

They both laughed. "Come on, Cor. Let's go through your mail before Quint gets here. I'm sorry I haven't had the time to come over before now and help you with it."

"Not a big deal. Let me grab my checkbook so we can take care of any bills that aren't paid electronically."

Corrie grabbed a light jacket from the hook in her closet where she kept it and followed Emily into the kitchen. She eased herself onto a stool and waited for Emily to shuffle through the envelopes.

"Trash, trash, ad flier—oooh, this looks interesting!"

"What is it?"

Emily laughed. "A catalog for sex toys."

Corrie shook her head at her friend. "Whatevs, come on, hurry up."

"In a hurry, Cor?"

"What time is it anyway?"

"You've got a bit before he's supposed to be here. Relax. Okay, let's see…cell phone auto payment notification, same for the electric and cable…when are you going to cancel your cable? Seriously, you never watch TV, it's a waste."

"I like the background noise sometimes."

"Oh…what's this?"

"What?"

"It's a letter."

"Well, no crap, Emily. They're all letters."

"No, I mean, it's a personal letter. You usually don't get letters from people."

Corrie didn't take offense. Emily was right. Anyone who knew her wouldn't write her a letter, and very few of her friends and family knew Braille, and none were proficient enough to write her an entire letter in the language. They stuck to the computer for their correspondence. "Who's it from?"

"I don't know, there's no return address."

"Fine, would you open it already then?"

She heard Emily tearing open the letter and then silence as she read it.

"Oh my God."

Corrie had never heard that tone of voice from her friend before. "What? What is it?" Corrie felt Emily's hand at her elbow, gently tugging her off the stool and out of the kitchen. "What? Emily, you're freaking me out."

"Quint's gonna be here soon, let's wait out here."

"Emily Brooks, you tell me right now what the heck is going on." Corrie dug her heels in and refused to take another step.

"It was a threatening letter."

"Threatening? What did it say?"

Before Emily could respond, there were two knocks on the door, a pause, then two more.

"It's Quint," Corrie said softly. "That's his special knock to let me know it's him." She walked over to the door and went through the same process she did the other night to verify his identity. It was better to be safe than sorry. When Quint confirmed it was him, Corrie opened the door.

"Hey, you look beautiful."

"Thanks." Her voice was reverent when she told him, "You smell divine."

He chuckled. "Is that your way of telling me I look nice?"

"Yeah, smell is kinda a big thing for me, for obvious reasons." When Corrie heard a throat being cleared behind her, she said, "Oh, sorry. This is Emily," and gestured to where she'd left her friend standing.

"Hi, Emily, it's nice to meet you. Corrie has talked a lot about you."

"Hi. Uh, Corrie, we need to tell him."

"Tell me what?"

"I don't think—"

Emily interrupted her. "She got a threatening letter."

Corrie thought she could actually feel the air around her change. She really hadn't wanted to do this now. She wanted to go on her date and put all the scary crap behind her for the night.

She sighed, knowing it was too late now. Darn it.

"Show me." Quint's words were clipped and urgent.

They all walked back into the kitchen. Corrie could hear Quint head over to the counter where they'd been going through her mail.

"I dropped it as soon as I realized what it was. It

was toward the bottom of the stack, so it probably came earlier this week. I haven't been able to get over here to help Corrie in about seven or so days. I'm so sorry, I should've been here sooner, I—"

"This isn't your fault, Emily. Don't blame yourself. I was over here the other night. I should've at least thumbed through it."

"Both of you, stop it," Corrie said firmly. "The only fault here is with the jerk who sent it. And Quint, if you'd started pilfering through my mail, I wouldn't have been happy."

Corrie could hear the humor in Quint's voice as he asked Emily, "Does she ever swear?"

"No. It's annoying as hell too. I keep telling her Ethan's too young to pick up on any bad words, but she still refuses to use adult words when she's pissed."

"Okay, you two. Quit. Quint, what should I do with it?"

"You don't need to do anything with it. I'll take care of it. Can you give me a few minutes to call my friend Dax and let him know what's up?"

"Uh, Dax... That's not the guy who was at the restaurant was it?"

"No, that was Cruz. Dax is with the Texas Rangers."

"But, I thought the police department was working the case?"

"They are, but we call in the Rangers when we need assistance in investigating cases. Because of the nature of what we're dealing with, and the fact we haven't been able to locate Shaun yet, Matt...err... Detective Algood, asked for assistance from the Rangers."

"Oh, okay. I guess we'll have to reschedule anyway."

Corrie heard Quint take a step toward her and then felt his hands on her shoulders. She looked up to where his face should be.

"This isn't going to end our date, Corrie. As soon as I take care of this, we're still going out," he said in an earnest voice. "I told you I wanted to take you on a date, so that's what I'm going to do."

"Okay, but just so you know, if it gets too late, I'm fine with doing it another day."

"It's not going to take very long, promise." He kissed her forehead, then stepped back, taking his hand with him. "Emily, I know we just met, but can I ask a huge favor?"

"Of course."

"Once Dax gets here, can you stay until he's done? I want to take my girl out."

"Of course. No problem."

"Emily," Corrie protested, "don't you have to get home to Bethany and Ethan?"

"No. They'll be fine. You've been looking forward to this date all week. I got this."

Corrie groaned in embarrassment. Please God, let the earth open and swallow her up. She heard Quint chuckle and knew she was turning red.

She felt his breath against her cheek then her ear as he leaned into her and whispered so only she could hear him, "Don't be embarrassed, I've been looking forward to taking you out all week too."

He then backed away and Corrie heard him walk to the other side of the kitchen.

"Holy hell, girlfriend. I'm sorrier than you'll ever know that you're going through this, but wow. That is one hunk of a man you've got there," Emily whispered.

"Really?" Corrie turned her back to Quint and kept her voice low so he couldn't hear their conversation.

"Really. If I wasn't in love with Bethany, you might have a fight on your hands."

"Whatever, you're so stupid in love with her you wouldn't look at anyone else, even if you *were* attracted to men. Can you describe him for me?"

Emily didn't even hesitate, having done this for her friend many times over the years. "He's taller than you are, with dark hair. It's got a bit of a wave in it and I'm sure it probably sticks up all over the place when he runs his hand through it. His dark against your blonde looks amazing. He's as muscular as anyone I've ever seen, except on TV, and he has some sort of kickass tattoo sticking out from under the right sleeve of his shirt." Emily wrapped it up. "He's got prominent cheekbones and a square jaw. Brown eyes, full lips, no piercings that I can see. In short? I might pitch for the other team, but I'm telling you, he's fucking *hot*."

Corrie chuckled and shook her head at her friend. She couldn't help but be pleased that Quint was good-looking. It wasn't that she put a lot of stock into a person's looks, because honestly, there were a lot of other factors that were way more important to her considering she couldn't even see him to appreciate what he looked like, but even without her sight, she could easily imagine how good-looking Quint was. Emily's description matched his voice to a T. She tried to play it down. "Whatever." Corrie's voice got sincere. "Thanks for being here for me, Em. Seriously. I love you."

"You're welcome. We're here for each *other*. Always. Never forget it. Whatever you need, whenever you need it."

"Come here." Corrie held out her arms and

smiled as Emily wrapped hers around her. They embraced and held on until Quint came back across the room to them. "You guys okay?"

Corrie pulled away, smiling. "Yeah. We're good."

"Okay. Emily, Dax should be here pretty quickly. He was already out finishing up an investigation. He said he'd swing by here and collect the letter. I know you know this, but don't touch the envelope again. We'll probably need you to come down to the station and give your fingerprints so we can exclude yours when examining it."

"No problem."

"Oh, but Em, what about that warrant for your arrest back in New York?" Corrie's voice was serious and urgent—and she waited a beat before succumbing to the smile she'd been holding back.

Emily burst into laughter and choked out, "Oh my God, Cor, you should've seen his face."

Corrie laughed along with her friend. It felt good to laugh and tease Quint. She and Emily used to play tricks on people all the time. Corrie knew she should probably be freaking out about the letter and the threat that obviously came with it, but she couldn't work up the energy. Her impending date with Quint was first and foremost in her thoughts at the moment. Later that night she'd probably freak out about the letter, but for now she was more excited about spending some time with Quint.

Frustrated that she probably wasn't going to have the luxury to not think about what it said, she resigned herself to seeing if she could get Quint or Emily to read it to her before they left. At least that way she'd get the worst of it over with. Then maybe, if the date went well, she could think about that rather than whatever the contents of the stupid note were.

"You'll pay for that, sweetheart," Quint mock threatened, putting his arms around her from behind.

Corrie leaned back against him, loving the feel of him along the length of her body. He was a few inches taller than she was, and because he wasn't wearing his uniform or bulletproof vest, she could feel his hard strength, so different from her own. She didn't dare back all the way into him, it was too soon for an intimacy like that, but she couldn't help but wonder if she aroused him at all.

Stopping those kinds of thoughts before they could strengthen, she asked, "Will you read me the letter, Quint?"

"No."

Corrie turned around and put her hands on her

hips, not expecting his quick, blunt response. "What? Why not?"

"You don't need to hear it."

"Yes, I do. It was addressed to *me*. And how can I keep myself safe if I don't know what I'm up against?"

"First of all, you won't have to keep yourself safe…you've got me, and the department, and all of my friends at your back. Secondly, I don't *want* you to hear it."

Corrie nodded. "I know you don't, I'm not doing cartwheels about it myself, but I'm not five years old. It's not like I'm going to lose any *more* sleep over it. I'm already not sleeping, imagining the worst. In some way, maybe this'll make me feel better. Make me feel like I'm not making up the creepy feeling crawling up the back of my neck each night. Please, Quint."

She heard him sigh. "I don't want to…but okay. We'll get it over with, but as soon as Dax gets here, I'm taking you out and we're going to forget all this for a night."

"Thank you."

Quint ground his teeth together as he walked back to the counter and to the letter lying there. It was written on a piece of lined paper torn from a notebook. The lettering was overdone, obviously camouflaged. It was short and to the point. He'd used a napkin earlier to turn the letter over so he could read it.

He looked at Corrie. She was standing tall, not looking worried at all, while her friend Emily looked completely freaked the hell out. The two women were holding hands, and with a second glance, Quint could tell that Corrie wasn't as calm as she might appear. Her hand was clutching Emily's so hard her knuckles were white.

Fuck. He hated this. He might as well get it over with.

"It says, '*We told you to keep quiet. You didn't. Hope your affairs are in order. Too bad you'll never see us coming.*'"

"It's a little dramatic isn't it?"

"Damn it, Corrie. This isn't a laughing matter."

Quint could see Corrie's mood shift.

"I know it's not. Darn it, Quint. I was in that room stuffed under the sink wondering if I'd live to see another minute. I heard my friends being killed. I was *there*. I know this isn't funny, no matter if whoever sent that thinks *they* are, with their little dig about my eyesight. But I can't lose it. If I lose it, they win. Whoever 'they' are. I have to be smart, use my head. They're trying to scare me, and it's working, but I can't let them get to me. I just can't."

Quint had her in his arms before she got the last word out. "You won't let them get to you. *I* won't let them get to you."

He absently heard Emily puttering around the apartment, obviously trying to stay out of their way. Finally he drew back and looked at Corrie. He ran one of his thumbs under her eye. "Dry. You don't cry easily, do you, sweetheart?"

She shook her head. "I just...I cried a lot as a child. I don't know why I don't now. It's hard to get completely worked up over things knowing how bad life can really be sometimes. Stubbing my toe hurts, or listening to a sad book or movie...but I have a hard time crying over those things when they're honestly superficial in my life."

"I'm going to do what I can to keep you safe," Quint told her, breezing over her comment about her lack of tears.

"Okay."

"I am."

"Can we talk about this later?"

Just as the words left Corrie's mouth, there was a knock at the door.

Emily rushed over to answer it as Quint stepped back from Corrie.

"Yeah, we'll talk about this later," he promised. He turned, keeping one hand on the small of Corrie's back. "Come on, that'll be my buddy. I want you to meet Dax. Someday I'll tell you the story of what happened to him and his girlfriend, Mackenzie."

After the introductions were over, Dax pulled on a pair of gloves and put the letter and envelope into a plastic bag and headed back to the door to leave.

"That's it?" Corrie asked incredulously. "You're not going to take fingerprints, or ask me any questions, or otherwise grill me about anything?"

"Yup, that's it…unless you've got any more notes stashed somewhere or have anything else pressing you want to tell me right this second?"

"Don't you want to hear what happened?"

His friend laughed. "Ms. Madison, it's clear you and Quint are on your way out. I'm happy to stand here and discuss this letter all night, but it looks like you have other plans. My buddy hasn't been on a date for a *very* long time and I'm fucking thrilled he's managed to get someone as pretty as you to agree to be seen in public with his ugly self."

Corrie could hear the affection for his friend in Dax's voice. She smiled as he continued, "I've also been working all day and I'd like to get home to Mack, my girlfriend. I'll catch up with you tomorrow, by phone if that's easier for you, or I'll get in touch with Detective Algood, if you're more comfortable talking to him. Either way, you both look too pretty to be cooped up in this apartment gabbing about something none of us can do anything about at the moment. Go out. Have fun."

Corrie looked up at where Quint was. "Is he always like that?"

"Fuck no. He's usually a pain in the ass and all about protocol. But I'm not looking a gift horse in the mouth. If he says to get out of here, I'm all for it."

"Okay, let me grab my jacket and purse."

"Here you go, Cor." Emily was there with her stuff. "I'm going too. This works out great. I can get home to Bethany and our son and eat with them."

The foursome walked out of the apartment and Corrie reset the alarm and locked her door. As soon as the door was locked and Corrie had put her key away, Quint took her hand in his to lead her to the car. They all walked down to the parking lot together. Quint gave Dax a chin lift and he returned it before heading to his vehicle and easing out of the lot.

"Call me tomorrow, Cor. I need to know what's going on and what we're doing next."

"*We* aren't doing anything, Em. I already told you, I'm not involving you any more than you already are."

"But—"

It was Quint who interrupted her this time. "I'll

be in touch, Emily. I agree with Corrie, though. You shouldn't be involved in this. I'll take care of your friend."

"Swear?"

"Swear."

"Okay…don't do anything I wouldn't do tonight then."

Corrie laughed out loud. "I don't think that's the best advice, knowing how much you love Bethany."

Quint watched the banter between Corrie and Emily with a grin. It was obvious that the two women were close. And the fact that Corrie wasn't prejudiced made him like her all the more. Every scrap of information he picked up about the woman standing next to him, seemingly content to hold his hand, solidified the warm feeling in his belly that she was meant to be his.

After Emily had gotten in her car and driven off, Quint returned his hand to the small of Corrie's back. He felt her arch against him just a bit and he smiled. "Come on, sweetheart. I have a dinner to take you to."

CHAPTER 7

CORRIE NERVOUSLY UNLOCKED HER DOOR, somehow managing not to drop her keys in the process. She could feel Quint standing at her side. He had one hand on her hip and she could feel his thumb caressing her side as he stood patiently, letting her unlock her apartment by herself.

It was one of the four hundred twenty-three thousand things she found herself mentally calculating that she liked about the man. Holding her hand as he helped her navigate? Check. Asking her if she read Braille, then requesting a Braille menu from the hostess? Check. After the waiter put down their drinks, moving hers until it touched her hand so she'd know where it was? Check. Calmly and without fanfare explaining, by using a typical clock face, where the food was on her plate? Check.

Even now, he could've been overbearing and asked for her keys so he could open her door for her, but he didn't. He got it. He really seemed to understand that she wasn't helpless because she couldn't see.

They'd talked a lot throughout dinner about how she got around and what assistive technologies she used in her everyday life. She promised to show him some of them when they got back to her place.

Now they were here. Corrie's heart beat quickly. He'd been touching her all night, and it was driving her crazy.

She finally got the door open and she keyed in the code to the alarm.

"Wait here while I go and check things out."

Without giving her a chance to argue, Quint was gone. If Corrie was honest with herself, she was glad he was here. She would've been very nervous to come back to her apartment by herself, especially after receiving that darn letter.

Quint was back within minutes. "It's all clear. Let me take your jacket."

Corrie turned and shrugged out of her jacket and felt Quint take it. "Where does it go?"

"What?"

"Where does it go?" Quint repeated easily.

"Just put it anywhere."

"No. Tell me where it goes. I'm not an idiot, Corrie. I can tell that every single thing in your apartment has its place. If I put it down somewhere, you won't find it as easily. Tell me where you'd put it if you came home alone."

Darn, she kept forgetting how observant he was. "In my closet in my room. The third hook on the right when you walk in."

"Be right back."

Corrie wandered into the kitchen as she heard Quint head down the hall to her bedroom. She fought a blush, thinking about him in her room. She'd just pulled the coffeepot to the edge of the counter when he returned.

"Do you want coffee?"

"Sure, if you'll have some with me."

Corrie nodded and reached for the water faucet. She held the carafe under the faucet until it was nearly full. Then she turned to the pot and opened the top and poured it into the reservoir. She put the now-empty glass pot on the burner on the machine and lifted out the little basket with used grounds in it. She opened the cabinet under the sink and dumped the grounds into the trash can.

Next, Corrie turned the water back on and ran the basket under it, rinsing the old grounds away.

Then she placed it back into the coffeemaker and grabbed the plastic bin of coffee grounds.

"I hope vanilla is okay?"

"It's perfect."

Corrie screeched in surprise as Quint's voice came from right beside her. "Holy cow, you scared me! I didn't realize you were right there." She laughed shakily. "That doesn't happen often, you know, I always hear people when they approach me."

"You were distracted. And I must say, you are absolutely fascinating to watch."

"What do you mean?" Corrie turned back to the coffee. She pulled out a spoon that she kept inside the plastic jug and scooped out a large spoonful. She managed not to jerk in surprise when she felt Quint's arms snake around her waist to rest right under her breasts. He held her loosely, but with control. The contradiction was arousing as hell.

"You know exactly where everything is. You didn't fill the pot too full, you got it right to the ten-cup line. You didn't hesitate to pour it into the right place on the coffeemaker. If I didn't know better, I'd think you were pulling my leg this entire time and you can see as well as I can."

Corrie tried to ignore the huge compliment Quint had given her without realizing it, but couldn't. "Thank you. Seriously. You have no idea what it means to someone like me when people don't realize I can't see." She continued with what she was doing, a little hesitantly now that she knew Quint was scrutinizing her so closely. She managed to get three scoops of the coffee grounds into the basket. She flipped the lid closed and turned the machine on. She soon heard the gurgling of the water making its way through the machine and the alluring smell of vanilla coffee wafted through the air.

"Show me some of the other assistive technologies you have in the kitchen," Quint demanded as he stepped back, giving her some room.

"Seriously?"

"Yeah. Everything about you amazes me."

Not knowing how to respond to that, Corrie reached over and opened a cabinet. She pointed to where she knew her measuring set was. "I have a Braille label maker. I've marked all of the measuring spoons and cups with their sizes. I really don't need them much anymore, I can tell by touch which cup is which.

"My salt and pepper shakers have Braille marks on the ridges so I know which is which without having to taste them. I have a boil alert disk that I put in the bottom of the pan when I'm boiling water. It rattles when the water starts boiling so I know it's time to put in the pasta or rice or whatever. I have talking meat thermometers; my kitchen timer, as you can see, has raised bumps for minutes and larger markings at five minutes and a big raised bar at an hour."

Corrie pointed to her right. "Even my microwave talks to me. And as you noticed, everything has its place, especially in the kitchen. Emily helps me when I need it, but I try to do most things myself. I order lots of food online so I don't have to worry about the grocery store, I label everything. Every now and then I'll open a can thinking I'm eating soup to find something else entirely." She laughed at herself. "The fridge is organized so I know what's in there and where it is. I sometimes forget about the expiration dates, but I've learned to sniff everything before I use it, just in case."

"Did I say you were amazing?"

"Uh, yeah, but it's not that big of a deal."

"I was wrong." Quint ignored her and kept on. "You're *fucking* amazing."

Corrie giggled a bit. "Actually, I'm probably considered on the extreme side of anal to most people."

"No. Not at all."

Corrie sobered a bit as she looked up at Quint. He'd taken her in his arms as she was explaining some of the things in her kitchen that helped her be independent. He'd clasped his hands at the small of her back and held her to him. Corrie could feel his hard thighs against hers and, if she wasn't mistaken, his hard length as well.

"I realize this isn't a normal way to live, Quint. No sighted person could live this way."

"Why not?"

"Why not? Because. Look at it. It's crazy. I know it is."

"Someone told you that, didn't they?"

Corrie paused before nodding in agreement.

"Come on." Quint took her hand and led her to her couch. Corrie didn't have the gumption at the moment to tell him he didn't need to lead her to her own couch, she knew where it was, but she enjoyed the feel of her hand in his. He pulled her to the couch, then sat. Corrie stood awkwardly for a moment before he pulled her down next to him. He settled her into his side as if they sat like that all the time.

Corrie could feel the beat of his heart under her hand. She resisted the urge to explore. She hadn't "seen" this man yet, the time hadn't been right to ask him if she could run her hands over him to see what he looked like. But now…it seemed right. Before she could ask, he spoke.

"Tell me."

"Tell you what?" Corrie was confused. What were they talking about?

"Tell me about the asshole who told you he couldn't live this way."

Corrie froze. How had he figured out that it was a *man* who'd told her that? When she'd agreed with him, she figured he'd think it was her parents or a friend who'd made the insinuation. She sighed softly. Damn Quint's observation abilities. She was silent for a moment, not knowing where to start.

"I don't bite. Go on."

"I know you don't. I was just trying to figure out where to start this sad tale of woe." Her voice came out just this side of snarky.

Quint laughed. "I love when you get like this. Go on then, take your time."

Corrie shook her head at the crazy man currently holding her in his arms. She could feel one of his arms around her back, resting on her hip. The other hand was resting over her own palm on his chest. He rubbed the back of her hand with his thumb. He smelled so damn good, and Corrie just wanted to bury her face in his neck and never come up for air, but he'd asked her a question. She wanted to tell him, to make him understand what life was like living with a blind person. Well, at least living with *her.* She supposed every person was different. Other people might not be as anal as she was. She didn't know. All she knew was that she wanted whatever it was they were doing to continue. She'd never felt so comfortable with someone so quickly before.

Corrie took a deep breath and started. The sooner she told him, the sooner it'd be over. "I was dating Ian for several months. We got along great. He was attentive, but not smothering. We used to play cards almost all night—"

"How do you play cards?"

"Are you going to let me tell this story or what?"

"Yeah, after you tell me how you play cards."

Corrie lifted her head and looked up where his voice was. "You're kinda annoying, you know that?"

"Yeah, so my friends tell me. Cards?"

"And persistent," Corrie grumbled, but gave in with a smile. "I ordered a couple decks of special cards off the Internet. They have both Braille and regular print on them so I can play with a sighted person without any issues. They're plastic and actually waterproof and are really cool. Not that I'd play cards in the shower or tub or anything, I just thought it was neat to have cards that could get wet and wouldn't get ruined."

"Huh, I never knew anything like that existed either. Strip poker in the rain...who knew. Okay, go on. Ian," Quint sneered his name, "was attentive, but not smothering."

Ignoring the obvious disdain in Quint's voice, Corrie continued her story. "Yeah, as I said, we got along well. I thought he loved me. I thought I loved him. He asked me to move in with him, I told him I couldn't, I was way too comfortable in my space, but I wouldn't mind if he moved in with me. He agreed. He moved in, was here about two weeks before leaving. We tried to keep dating after he moved out, but it wasn't the same. He admitted to me that he'd had no idea living with a blind person was so...'exhausting' was the word I think he used."

"Exhausting? What the fuck does that mean?"

"I think he meant what I showed you. Everything has a place. The kitchen drove him especially crazy. He told me once it reminded him of that movie with Julia Roberts where she's being stalked by a crazy ex...*Sleeping with the Enemy*. He hated that all my food was lined up precisely and I'd spend at least an hour after shopping labeling it all. He'd leave his shoes in the middle of our bedroom and I'd trip over them. I once hit my head on the corner of my little table and Em told me I had a huge bruise for days."

Quint growled, and Corrie felt the rumble under her hand resting on his chest, but he didn't say anything, so she tried to finish up her story quickly.

"I tried to show Ian where I'd made room in my closet for his shoes and things to go. He whined that he was tired and it was hard to put everything in a specific place every single time. The last straw was the time I accidently started a small grease fire. I heard the whoosh of the flames and felt the heat on my face, and reached for the baking soda, but he'd moved it the last time he was in the kitchen when he was doing something else. I was yelling at him to come and help me because I couldn't find the darn stuff and the fire almost got out of control. I kinda lost my temper and told him off. I told him how important it was that he not move things without telling me. He got pissed, we said some unforgivable things to each other, and he left that day."

"Prick."

"What?"

"I said he was a prick."

Corrie sighed sadly. "No, he really wasn't. It's mostly my fault, honestly. It's impossible for someone who can see to understand the importance of needing to know where things are."

"Corrie, you're wrong. If he'd come to you and said, 'Hey, I bought some spices and I'd like to put them in the cabinet where the baking soda is, can you come help me figure out how to organize everything so you know where it is,' would you have gotten mad and refused?"

"What kind of question is that?" Corrie questioned testily. "No, of course not. I don't really care *where* things are, as long as I can find them when I need them. I don't want to put sugar in my food when I think it's really salt."

"Exactly."

"Quint, you're confusing the ever-loving daylights out of me. Exactly what?" Corrie felt Quint lean in closer to her. She could feel his breath on her face as he spoke earnestly.

"It's not that you're opposed to moving things around, you just want to know where they are."

"Yeah, that's what I said."

"So, if I said, 'Hey, I want to move the couch so it's under the window and put the chair in the other corner'…what would you say?"

"Sure. Whatever. It's not like I can say it doesn't look as good where you want it. I can't see it anyway. It's knowing where it is that's important. "

Corrie startled as Quint eased her backward until she was lying on her back on the couch. She could feel him crouched over her. "Quint! What are you doing?" She reached up and found his chest. She put both hands against it and held on.

"You're not anal, Corrie."

She snorted at him.

"You're not. You don't care where things are. You don't care what's in here. You just care *where* it is so you don't run into it or so you can find it again."

"That's what I've been telling you," Corrie told him, confused, wondering where he was going with his observations and feeling like they were talking in circles.

"Living with you wouldn't be exhausting. It would simply mean communication, compromise and, the caveman part of me wants to say, protection as well."

Corrie didn't know what to say, so she kept quiet. Quint didn't seem to mind as he continued.

"If you were mine, and I was living here with you, I'd see it as my duty to put things back where they belonged. It would be my way of protecting you. How much of a selfish bastard would I be to move furniture without telling you, or to leave my shit in the middle of the floor where you could trip over it and get hurt? I'm not saying it wouldn't take some getting used to, but I honestly don't see it as that big of a deal."

Corrie felt Quint's hand on her cheek. "You're normal, Corrie. As normal as anyone else. Just because you can't see doesn't mean you're anal or 'exhausting.' You're just you. You deserve love as much as anyone else."

"I don't know what to say," Corrie told him honestly after digesting his words.

"That's a first."

Corrie huffed out a laugh, then got serious again. "Can I touch you?"

"Touch me?" Quint's voice deepened as he said the words.

Corrie laughed nervously. "I didn't mean that... exactly. I don't know what you look like. I mean, Emily described you a little to me tonight, but I'd like to see for myself. I know what you smell like, how tall you are, that you have this wonderful, deep growly voice and that you're muscular, but I have no idea what you *look* like."

"Is this a deal breaker?"

"Are you nervous?" Corrie couldn't believe Quint could be sensitive about his looks.

"A little. I mean, you're gorgeous. I'm not in your league at all. You might take one look at my crooked nose and kick me to the curb."

Corrie giggled. "As if. Emily told me you were freaking hot."

"I bet she didn't say 'freaking.'"

Corrie laughed then inhaled sharply as Quint rolled, careful to keep a firm grasp on her waist so she didn't fall off the couch. He held her to him until he'd switched their positions. He lay under her and Corrie straddled his hips. There was no way he could hide his erection from her, as she was currently perched right on top of it, but he didn't think she'd mind. At least he hoped not. He stretched his arms up and put them under his head. "Have at it, sweetheart."

CHAPTER 8

CORRIE DIDN'T HESITATE in case Quint changed his mind. She loved getting to know people this way, but didn't often get the chance. It wasn't like she could put her hands all over people when they first met.

She put her hands on Quint's chest and ran them down to his waistline, then back up to his neck. She splayed her fingers and did it again. She then ran her hands over his shoulders and down his arms, gripping his muscles as she explored.

"You're very muscular."

"Um-hummm."

Corrie didn't pause in her perusal, but noted his lack of response vaguely. She squeezed his biceps and barely held back a groan. His arms were huge... and immensely sexy.

"Emily told me you have a tattoo. What's it of?"

"It's not that exciting."

Corrie smiled and teased, "A naked woman? A naked man? A giant octopus wrapping its tentacles around your arm and down your back?"

Quint laughed and Corrie could feel his chest rumbling under her hands. "It's an American Flag with writing on it."

"There has to be more to it than that," Corrie groused. "I'll never be able to see it. Please describe it for me. I want to picture it in my head."

"It's big, about six inches long. It goes from the top of my arm to the middle of my bicep. Some of it can be seen when I wear a short-sleeve shirt, like right now. On the red stripes, I had the artist add in cursive a phrase I wrote when I graduated from the police academy: Honor those who have fallen. Protect those who are weak. Serve those who need help. Always remember those less fortunate."

Corrie pictured it in her head. It was probably sexy as all get out...patriotic and hot at the same time. She was sorry she'd never see it. "You said you wrote that? It's beautiful. Does it have a deeper meaning?"

"Deeper meaning?"

"Yeah, I mean, I get that it's about your service to

our country and all…but I have a feeling there's more to it."

Quint brought his hands down from his head and rested them on her hips. He ran his thumbs over the skin under the hem of her top as he spoke. "I told you that I'd always wanted to be a cop. From the time I was a little boy until I decided to major in Criminal Justice in college, it was the only thing I ever wanted to do. Graduating from the police academy was one of the most monumental things I'd ever done in my life. I felt like my true life was just starting. I wanted to commemorate it, to wear ink that would always remind me of why I'm in this profession. I doodled those words on a napkin one night and they stuck with me. It's my mantra, so to speak."

His words gave Corrie goose bumps. She'd never felt that strongly about anything before. She was impressed and honored Quint had shared the story behind his tattoo with her. "I love it. I bet it's beautiful." She rubbed up and down his biceps, enjoying the feel of his muscles flexing under his shirt below her hands.

"Want me to take off my shirt?" Quint tried to change the topic…and get to the good stuff.

"Yeah, but I thought it might be weird if I asked this soon. I mean, we just had our first date tonight."

"We might've had our first date tonight, but we've been talking a lot before that."

"You wouldn't mind, then?"

"Hell no, sweetheart. I wouldn't mind."

Corrie felt Quint shift under her as he removed his T-shirt and then she felt his warm, muscular skin under her hands. "How are you always warm?" She'd asked it as a rhetorical question, but he answered her anyway.

"My body temperature has always run a bit warmer than ninety-eight point six."

"Interesting, mine has always run a bit cold."

"We're a good match."

"Maybe so." Corrie was fascinated with the ridges and muscles of Quint's chest. She ran her hands over his pectoral muscles again and grinned when his nipples peaked under her fingers. "You like that." It wasn't a question.

"Sweetheart, having your hands on me is beyond exciting. I feel I should warn you…if you keep that up you might bite off more than you can chew here."

"Sorry," Corrie said, not meaning it at all. She couldn't hold back the smile on her face. She felt the back of Quint's finger trail down her cheek.

"I like to see you smile."

"It's you. You make me smile."

"Good."

Corrie scooted forward a bit until she was straddling Quint's lower stomach instead of his hips, so she could more easily reach his face. She brought her hands up to where she thought his head was and paused.

"Don't stop now, Corrie. Go on. See me."

She did as Quint requested. Her fingertips feathered over his cheekbones, then up to his eyebrows. She felt him close his eyes and she learned the shape of them. She brought her fingers down to his nose and felt the bump he'd mentioned earlier. "It's not so bad…I'm sure it makes you look…rugged or something."

Corrie felt his lips curl up into a smile, but he didn't say anything. She continued her exploration at his lips. She traced his upper, then his lower lip with the tip of her finger, laughing when he pretended to bite at her. Bringing both hands back into play, she brought them up each side of his face and traced both ears, then ran them though the hair on his head.

Finally, after she'd explored and traced every inch of his face and head, he drawled, "So…do I pass inspection?"

"Yeah, you're cute."

"Cute?" he mock grumbled, bringing his hands up from her hips and tickling her sides. She screeched and tried to buck off him, but Quint had a tight hold on her. Finally he stopped torturing her and they both lay on the couch smiling.

"Can I massage your back?"

"Huh?" That wasn't what Quint expected Corrie to say at all.

"Can I give you a massage?"

"Really?"

"Yeah. You know I'm a chiropractor, I'm good at it. I promise."

"Sweetheart, anytime you want to rub my back, I'll be all for it."

"Good, we need to get on the floor though. The sofa is too soft."

Corrie stood up, giving Quint room to get up as well.

"I'm going to move the coffee table up against the wall, giving us more room. It'll be about four feet farther back than where it is now. You okay with that?"

Corrie smiled at Quint, loving how he tried to keep her safe from hurting herself. "That's great. Thanks."

Corrie heard Quint move the table, then lie on the ground. "I'll be right back, okay? I'm going to go get some lotion."

"Sure, I'll be riiiiight here where you left me."

Corrie giggled, knowing she sounded like a silly schoolgirl. She rushed off toward her bedroom and grabbed her vanilla lotion, knowing it was the least girly smelling stuff she had. She came back to the living room and to Quint's side. She popped open the top of the bottle. "You ready for this?"

"Give it your best shot."

Corrie grinned and got to work.

Thirty minutes and two sore hands later, Quint was a pile of goo under her. She'd worked his back muscles, massaging out all the kinks and knots she could find. She was glad she could help ease some of his pain, but if she was being honest with herself, she enjoyed having her hands all over him just as much.

"Feel good?"

"I might never move again. I'll just take up residence here on your floor and you can throw me a hotdog every now and then to keep me alive."

"I take it you enjoyed it."

Quint turned suddenly until he was on his back and Corrie was straddling his hips again. She felt his hard erection under her and gasped.

"As you can tell, I enjoyed it. Probably too much." He brought one of Corrie's hands up to his face and nuzzled into it. "I'd like to thank you properly."

Corrie's heart leapt as if she'd just run a two-mile

race. She wasn't sure what he had in mind, but whatever it was…she wanted it.

She nodded, figuring he'd see her. She felt his hands cup her cheeks and draw her down onto him. She caught herself with her hands on the floor by his shoulders and eagerly leaned down.

Quint looked at the beautiful woman over him. Her blond hair had partly come out of the clip that was holding it back and her face was flushed. He could smell the vanilla lotion she'd used on him. It permeated the air around them.

He gripped the sides of her neck with his hands and brought her slowly down toward him. He didn't want to rush her if she wasn't ready, but when she came down to him eagerly, he smiled. Thank God.

"I'm going to kiss you, Corrie. In light of our conversation the other night at your door, I wanted to make sure I didn't surprise you."

"Please, Quint."

His lips settled on hers and he heard a small gasp leave her mouth. Quint took advantage and plunged his tongue between her lips. He licked and sucked and learned her taste. Needing some air, he paused to take a breath. Corrie began to pull back, probably thinking the kiss was over, but Quint knew he'd not had enough of her yet. He turned them until Corrie was under him. She didn't stiffen in his embrace at all, but eagerly strained upward toward him.

Quint ran one hand down her neck, between her breasts and to her belly, then back up. He continued the dual assault, one hand on her body and his lips on her mouth, until she moaned under him. He lifted his mouth off hers. He needed to talk to her, or else he'd end up taking her right there on the floor…and he wanted more than that for both of them.

"Will you teach me to read Braille?"

"What?" Her confusion was adorable. Quint knew he'd lobbed that one at her out of left field, but he suddenly wanted to know everything about her. It probably wasn't fair to break off the hottest kiss he'd had in a long time to blurt it out, but being around Corrie made him want to be a better person…for *her*. He wanted to belong in her world as much as he was beginning to feel as if she belonged in his.

"I want to learn to read Braille. I know I'll never be as good at it as you are, but I want to do this with you."

"No one has ever asked me that before," she said with a hitch in her voice, obviously still lost in their kiss.

Quint waited until she'd worked though his request in her brain.

Finally she nodded, "Okay, if you really want to, I'll teach you Grade 1 Braille."

"What's Grade 1? Is that like first-grade Braille for kids?" he asked, genuinely confused.

"You really want to talk about this now?"

Quint smiled at the frustration in her voice. It wasn't the best time or place, but he felt the need to be as close to her as possible, and this was one way to do it. He ran his hand over her hair and tucked a piece behind her ear. "Humor me."

"Grade 1 isn't an elementary school grade; it's where every letter of the alphabet is expressed in a Braille pattern. Like, one dot is an A, two is a B, and so on. But I have to warn you, there aren't a lot of books or stuff written in Grade 1 because it's kinda tedious. Grade 2 is when some cells of Braille are used individually or in combination with other cells to form words or phrases."

"Can you give me an example?"

"It's hard to tell you and not show you, but for example, the Grade 1 cell for the letter Y is also the word 'you' in Grade 2 Braille."

"I get it. So it's kinda shorthand. I can learn the individual letters, but in more advanced Braille, a letter might represent a full word in Grade 2. Cool."

Corrie chuckled under him. "You say that now—"

Her words were cut off as Quint's mouth came

down on hers again. He didn't warn her it was coming or tease this time, but tilted her face to what he deemed was a perfect angle and devoured her. Their tongues tangled together and he alternated thrusting in and out, and then drawing back and nipping and caressing her lips.

Between kisses, Corrie begged, "Close your eyes."

"Why? I want to see you, you're beautiful." Quint hated the sadness that crossed her face for a split second before she blanked it. "Oh shit, that was insensitive of me. I'm sorry, Corrie."

"Don't be sorry. I'm glad you like the way I look. I don't want you to constantly watch what you say around me. I've been blind my whole life, Quint, I'm not going to get offended or burst into flames if you say 'I see' around me."

Ignoring her words, Quint told her evenly, "My eyes are closed."

"What?"

Quint brought her hand up to his face and drew it over his now closed eyes. "My eyes are closed. Talk to me."

Corrie cleared her throat and tried to hold back the tears she claimed she never shed anymore. He was so sweet to humor her. "What do you smell?"

"You."

"Be more specific."

Quint leaned into her and buried his nose in her neck and inhaled loudly. He smiled when Corrie giggled. "I smell vanilla. The lotion you used to massage my back."

"Anything else?"

"Lavender."

"That's my shampoo. Good job. Now kiss me."

"Gladly."

Quint kept his eyes shut and leaned down. He missed her lips the first time and they both giggled. He quickly righted his aim and kissed her hard again. It was different somehow this time. More intense. He'd certainly kissed women with his eyes closed before, but this time he actually thought about using his other senses while he did it. Without sight, everything seemed... more. He could taste the coffee she'd had after dinner, and the smell of the vanilla lotion filled his nose and made her even taste like vanilla, if that was possible. It was weird...and completely awesome.

He lifted his head and felt Corrie's hand on his face.

"Your eyes are still closed," she whispered, as if she'd expected him to cheat.

"Yeah."

"So?"

"It was more intense. I had to use all my other senses to experience the kiss."

"All those shows and books on BDSM know what they're talking about when they discuss the use of blindfolds."

Quint chuckled and finally opened his eyes. "I can't say I've read many romances about BDSM, and while I do admit to watching some porn, that's not really my thing. But it certainly makes for a more intense experience."

They were quiet for a moment and Quint ran his fingers over Corrie's face one more time. "We should get off the floor."

"Probably."

It was obvious Corrie wasn't going to move, so Quint eased himself up until he was on his knees and grabbed her hands. He helped her sit, then moved them both up and back onto the couch. He pulled her into his arms, loving the feel of her against his bare chest, and held her tight.

"For the record, Corrie Madison, I like you."

She smiled against his shoulder. "I like you too, Quint Axton."

"Glad we have that covered."

They sat in silence, until the automated voice from the clock in Corrie's room announced it was eleven o'clock.

"I have to get going," Quint said reluctantly.

"Do you want to stay?"

Quint almost groaned. Did he want to stay? Oh yeah, but he couldn't. He didn't want to rush her. He was enjoying the dating game they were playing. He hadn't played it since he was in high school. The one step forward, two steps backward dance they were doing was much more interesting and intense than most of the adult relationships he'd had. The women he'd been dating didn't bother playing games, but instead told him outright they wanted to sleep with him. But the dating game with Corrie was fun, different. Besides that, she looked almost embarrassed she'd said the words, and the last thing he wanted was for her to regret anything they did together.

"Yes, I want to stay, but I'm not."

"You're not?" Corrie sat up against him.

"Retract your claws, woman," he said with a laugh.

Corrie gasped and unclenched her hands, which had fisted into his chest when he'd said he wasn't staying. "Sorry."

Quint flattened his hand over hers and rubbed her with this thumb. "There's nothing more that I want to do than take you to your bed, strip you naked, and taste you from your toes to your luscious lips…" He heard her inhale sharply, and he smiled. "But I don't want to rush you."

"Rush me, Quint. I'm okay with that."

He kissed her hard, forcing her head back until she gasped and surrendered against him. He lifted his head and ran a fingertip over her plump just-kissed lips. "I don't want to rush this because I want it to last. I want *us* to last. I want you to get to know me. I want to get to know you better. I want to fall in like with you before I take you to bed and fall in love with you."

"F-fall in love with me?"

"Yeah, 'cos I can see it happening. I'm not there yet, but I don't want to rush what we're doing and not get the chance to see what we could become."

"I think I'm already falling in like with you, Quint."

He smiled down at her. "Good. Then my master plan is working. Come on, walk me to the door then lock up behind me."

"Okay."

Quint put his shirt back on and pulled the table back to where it was when he'd arrived. He looked around, making sure nothing else was out of place.

"What are you doing?" Corrie asked, standing by the kitchen counter.

"I'm making sure everything's put away." Quint

finished examining her space and came up to where Corrie was and saw a weird look on her face. "What's wrong now?"

"You were really trying to see if anything was out of place?"

"Of course. I don't want to leave anything out where you could get hurt if you ran into it."

"I think Emily and Bethany are the only ones that have done that before…but usually it's because they've brought over all of Ethan's baby stuff and the place is a disaster area by the time they're ready to leave."

Quint leaned down and kissed her hard again. "I'm glad to help."

She smiled up at him. "Thanks for making me forget everything for a night."

"You're welcome, sweetheart. Text me tomorrow? Let me know what you're up to?"

"I will. I'll call the station in the morning about the letter and see what's up."

"Good. Why don't you come with Emily when she comes in to give her fingerprints? Let me know when you'll be there and I'll try to come and meet you. We can talk about what the detective found out and perhaps come up with a plan. Maybe we can do lunch afterwards?"

"I'd like that."

"Will Bethany come too? She's more than welcome."

"Probably not. She's been staying at home and watching Ethan while Emily is at work. She's taking some time off of work to be with him. I'm not sure they'll want to bring him to a police station. They're a little overprotective. Especially Bethany. I swear she wouldn't even let me hold him if she thought she'd get away with it."

Quint chuckled. "Okay, I'm sure I'll meet her at some point."

"You want to?"

"Of course I do. She's your friend's partner. Why wouldn't I?"

"I've told you that I liked you tonight, haven't I?"

He smiled. "Yeah, but you can tell me again."

"I like you."

Quint brought Corrie into his arms and hugged her tightly. "Stay safe, Corrie. Don't let anyone in this apartment if you don't know who they are."

"I won't."

"Okay. I'll see you tomorrow." Quint kissed Corrie on the forehead, not trusting himself to stop if he touched his lips to hers again.

"Bye, sweetheart."

"Bye, Quint."

For the third time, Quint listened as Corrie

locked herself into her apartment. He only wished he could stay there and keep her safe. He hadn't earned the right yet, but he hoped it'd be soon.

* * *

THE MAN KEPT a keen eye on the door from his hiding spot as the cop left the blind bitch's apartment. He pulled out his cell and made a call.

"He's gone."

"I want that whore eliminated," the voice on the other end of the phone growled.

"The pig is becoming an issue. We need to wait."

"You know what? It's not about the cops or the fucking FBI. She's a pain in my ass and I *want* her eliminated," the other man insisted.

The man in the parking lot took another drag off his cigarette before speaking. "She's got a security system and is dating a fucking cop. I told you that letter was a bad idea. She's got more protection now than she had right after I did the job. We need to back the fuck off and let everyone chill. I can get to her a lot easier if everyone thinks the threat is over."

"I thought you wanted to grab her now and fuck her up?"

"I *did*, I *do*, but there's too much heat on her now. And when they don't find Shaun, they're gonna step up their game and there will be even more heat on her…and you and your operation."

"No, there won't. That asshole will be just another missing person. No one is ever gonna find his body. You made sure of that."

The man in the parking lot sighed quietly. He'd made his case. He could probably get to the blind chick if the boss insisted, but he hoped he'd see it his way.

He wanted her, all right. She wasn't fat, her tits would squeeze nicely in his hands, and he'd love to stick his cock inside her, but at the moment there was just too much attention around her. He didn't say anything and the boss man on the other end of the line continued.

"Fine, we'll do it your way…for now. But you stay on her. If it looks like they're closing in on my operation, end her. Got it?"

"Yes, sir."

The man stubbed out his cigarette under his boot and pocketed his phone after ending the call. Good. His way. He fucking liked his way. The poor little blind girl didn't have a chance in hell of getting away from him. He just needed to keep watch and figure out the best way to get to her…without causing her to alert anyone. He'd be patient. When it came to killing, he was always patient as long as, in the end, people ended up with their brains blown out. If he played with her a bit before he killed her...no one would be the wiser. Besides, he'd never fucked a blind chick.

He adjusted his pants over his erection and faded back into the shadows.

CHAPTER 9

CORRIE HELD on to Emily's elbow as they walked to the table in the small restaurant. Her cane dangled by her side just in case, but she usually didn't need it when she was with Emily and Bethany.

They loved Kona Grill. It was an eclectic restaurant that had everything from sushi to burgers. It'd been about a week and a half since her date with Quint, and Emily couldn't wait to give her the third degree anymore. They'd talked about Quint over the phone and after their first date, but Corrie knew she'd be grilled tonight by both Emily and Bethany. Which was okay; it meant they cared about her…and that they were simply nosy. They'd planned it so they'd have time for some girl talk before Quint got there.

Corrie was nervous for Quint to meet Emily and Bethany together. Oh, he'd already met Emily on the night of their first date, but for some reason it seemed different since he'd be meeting and talking with them together as a couple. Corrie didn't care about the fact that they were *together*-together, but this was Texas. Not exactly the most progressive state.

Emily was her best friend. She'd always been there for her. If Quint didn't get along with Emily— or Bethany—their relationship would be over before it began. And she really *really* wanted their relationship to continue.

The other night she and Quint had spent two hours talking about nothing in particular on the phone. It was nice to get to know him and ask him things that she would've felt embarrassed asking about face-to-face. He, in turn, felt comfortable to question her about her blindness. Corrie had no problem whatsoever telling him whatever he wanted to know, even if his questions weren't necessarily politically correct. It was obvious he was asking because he was curious and not out of maliciousness.

Quint had gotten off work in the afternoon then was doing some shooting practice with some of the other officers in the department and wouldn't be able to get to the restaurant until around six-thirty. Emily had picked her up at the clinic at five and the plan was for them to go to the restaurant, and meet Bethany there. Since Quint was meeting them later, he'd told them to go ahead and order and not to wait for him; he'd grab something as soon as he got there.

"Hey! Em! Over here!"

Corrie heard Bethany's voice carry over the din of the other diners. Emily steered them toward her. Corrie dropped her friend's arm when she stopped at their table and listened as Emily and Bethany greeted each other.

"How's my little man?" Emily cooed to Ethan.

Corrie smiled. She loved how gushy Emily got whenever she was around her son.

"How was he today?" Emily asked her partner.

"Good," Bethany preened. "He really is a perfect baby. He did his normal baby stuff today…ate, slept, and pooped."

They all laughed. Corrie settled into the chair Emily had stopped her beside and put her elbows on the table.

"So…" Bethany started. "Corrie, Em tells me you've snagged yourself one hot hunk of a man."

"I don't know about that, but so far he seems pretty darn near perfect."

"We'll see." Her tone was skeptical.

"Bethany!" Emily scolded. "Don't go chasing him off tonight. He really did seem like a good guy when I met him."

"I know, but again, I'm reserving judgment. I don't care if he seems to be as nice as Mr. Rogers himself...I have to see it for myself. You know I'm protective of those I love, Em."

Corrie smiled as she heard her friends kiss briefly.

"So...how's he in bed?" Bethany asked nonchalantly.

Corrie about choked on the water she'd just picked up. "I don't know...yet. But if he makes love as well as he kisses, I'm sure it'll be fantastic."

"You haven't slept with him yet?" Emily asked.

"Uh, no," Corrie said in a drawled incredulous voice. "It's only been a week and a half since our date. And besides, he's kinda in on my case. You know, the whole bad-guy-threatening-me thing."

"Pbsst."

Corrie could picture Emily waving her hand in the air as she airily dismissed her words. "The looks that man was giving you as you left for dinner last week were smokin' hot. I can't believe he hasn't locked you in his room and made passionate love to you all night long."

"Emily!"

"What?" Her voice was amused.

Corrie shook her head. "You're impossible. Please don't embarrass me tonight."

"Would I do that?"

"Yes!"

They all laughed.

The waitress chose that moment to come up to the table. The trio had been to the restaurant so many times they didn't even need to see the menu anymore.

"I'd like the jambalaya, please." Emily always ordered the spicy seafood dish.

"Lobster mac and cheese."

Corrie smiled. Bethany's weakness was carbohydrates, and she always splurged whenever they went out. She was still trying to lose some of the baby weight she'd gained while carrying Ethan, but she'd probably run about ten miles tomorrow to take care of the extra calories she'd consume tonight. She'd never seen anyone able to eat and drink as much as Bethany did, and still be able to retain her slim figure.

"I'll take the big kahuna cheeseburger."

"I have no idea how you manage to eat that thing without getting it all over you," Emily complained good-naturedly. "Seriously, that thing is huge and drips with all the condiments they put on it. You're the neatest blind person I've ever met. It's annoying."

"You love me and you know it."

Corrie felt Emily lightly punch her in her arm teasingly. "I do, you crazy bitch."

They all laughed and fell into a comfortable conversation about work, catching up with their lives in general, and even Ethan's bowel movements and eating habits.

"I can't believe we're sitting here talking about poop and what the best way to pulverize food into infant-sized chunks is. What happened to us? We used to be cool!" Corrie teased her friends. When they started to defend themselves, Corrie held up a hand. "Okay, maybe we were never really cool in the first place. But seriously, I'm so happy for you two. With all that's stacked up against not only you having a relationship together, but also the prejudice against raising your son in today's society, I'm thrilled to be in both your lives. And I know I've told you this before, but I'll never do anything to put any of you in danger. I'd rather die than lead the guy who killed Cayley and the others to your door."

Corrie felt a hand on her own. "I might give you crap, but Corrie, I know how much you love Emily and Ethan." Bethany's words were heartfelt and as serious as Corrie had ever heard. "I never dreamed

I'd find a woman to love like Emily. And as sure as I stand here, I never thought I'd be a mother. Ethan means everything to me. I'd do whatever it took to keep him safe. If Satan himself walked into our house and told me to choose between my life and Ethan's, I'd choose Ethan every time. So I get what you're saying, and as Emily's wife, and as Ethan's mom, and as your friend…thank you. Seriously."

Corrie knew she had the goofiest grin on her face, but she couldn't help it. "We're so sappy, aren't we? What happened to us being cool?"

"We were never cool," Emily laughed. "You said it yourself!"

"True!"

The three women ate their meals when they arrived and ordered a round of some frou-frou drink the waitress recommended. They were laughing and reminiscing over stories when Bethany said in a quiet voice, "Don't look now, but there's a hottie coming straight for the table, and he can't take his eyes off of you, Corrie. I'm assuming your Quint has arrived."

Corrie turned in the direction from which she'd arrived at the table in and smiled. She felt a hand on her upper back, right before she smelled Quint's unique scent. His lips touched her temple then he spoke in his deep voice, which never failed to send a shiver down her spine. "Emily. Good to see you again. And you must be Bethany."

Corrie could picture in her head Quint holding out his hand for Bethany to shake.

"Hi. We've heard a lot about you."

"And I've heard nothing but good things about you, Bethany. And this little guy too."

Corrie lost the feel of Quint's hand as he went over to Ethan and cooed at him. Before too long he was back at her side, and Corrie heard the empty chair next to her being pulled out from the table and then Quint settle in beside her.

"Hi, sweetheart. Did you have a good day?" Quint's voice was breathy and intimate right next to her ear.

Corrie turned to face Quint. "Yeah. It feels good to get back into the swing of things at the clinic."

"All was quiet?"

Corrie knew what he meant. They'd talked at length regarding the reservations she had about returning to the clinic. He'd played devil's advocate and had given her lots of reasons not to return to work, but in the end told her he'd support her no matter what she decided as long as she was careful about her security.

She nodded at his question. "Yeah, nothing out of the ordinary happened. No calls, no letters, no firebombs." She smiled when she said the last and she felt Quint's finger stroke down her cheek.

"Good, that's good."

"How was your day?"

"Same old, same old. Two reports of burglaries, one cat stuck in a tree, and twelve speeding tickets."

"Only twelve? You're slipping."

Corrie heard Quint chuckle before Bethany interrupted them.

"Oh my Lord, you guys are so fucking cute it's almost sickening."

"Bethany! You can't swear in front of Ethan!" Corrie turned and scolded in what was a recurring argument between them.

"Just because *you* gave up swearing, doesn't mean I did."

"But you're his mom," Corrie said, appalled. "You can't swear around him either! You're supposed to be peeved when other people do."

"Cor, I think a few swear words are gonna be the least of this kid's issues as he grows up. And you know it."

Corrie knew what Bethany was talking about. Society was changing, but it didn't mean it'd be easy growing up in an unconventional family environment. "Yeah, well, regardless, he shouldn't grow up to be a potty-mouth…so his Aunt Corrie will be swear-free around him."

The others all laughed at her righteous indignation.

"So…Quint…"

Corrie groaned, knowing Bethany was starting her inquisition.

"What're you doing about this asshole who's threatening our Corrie? You got any more leads on the case? 'Cos I'll tell ya right now, me and Emily are not likin' it one bit."

"I'm right there with you, Bethany. What I'm doing is working with the detective on the case to dig up as much as we can on this Shaun guy. My friend on the Texas Rangers and my other friend in the FBI are also working as hard as they can to shut this shit down. We're not there yet, but I'll tell you this, I'll do everything I can to keep Corrie safe. You have my word."

There was silence around the table for a moment and Corrie just knew Bethany was giving Quint her "bitch face." She was about to open her mouth to try to say something…anything to break the tension, when Bethany spoke.

"Okay then. Good."

Introductions had been made, the tension had eased, and Corrie was able to relax as her friends continued to chat about nothing in particular and get to know Quint.

He was amazing. Corrie felt his hand on the back of her chair as they talked. He'd occasionally play with a strand of her hair and rub his thumb on the back of her neck. Even though he wasn't talking to her specifically, Corrie knew Quint's attention was on her.

She tried to imagine what Quint saw in her friends. Emily was thirty-four and Bethany was twenty-five. Emily sometimes complained that she felt like a cougar when people gave them weird looks. They were about the same height, five-six or so, but very different in looks. Emily had crazy curly black hair that she was always complaining about being in her way, but Corrie knew was probably beautiful and lush. Bethany was slender and blonde. Even though she looked harmless and cute and kinda like a pixie, Corrie knew firsthand she could be a complete hardass. She might have gotten past being the one to start fights, but if someone else did, she was one-hundred percent in. Corrie loved them both. They were as good friends as anyone could ever have.

"Okay, kids. I hate to break this party up, but Ethan's getting restless and we need to get him home," Emily stated during a lull in the conversation. "Corrie? You coming with us? We can drop you off."

"I'll take her." Quint's voice was lazy, but firm.

"It's not a big deal," Emily said. "Her place is on our way home."

"It's fine. I'm happy to drop her off. You guys need to get that little guy home."

Corrie could hear Ethan kicking and gurgling in his carrier. When Emily started to protest again, Corrie kicked where she thought her leg might be under the table to shut her up.

"Ow! Shit, Corrie. I have no idea how you always know right where my leg is!"

Corrie knew she was blushing. Darn Em for calling her out.

Quint laughed. "Come on, sweetheart. I'm sure you have to be tired."

They all packed up their stuff and stood from the table. Corrie felt Quint's arm go around her waist as he steered her through the tables to the front of the restaurant. When they got to the door, he shifted and took her hand in his, as he always did. Corrie squeezed his hand lightly in thanks.

"It was good meeting you, Quint," Bethany said seriously. "You seem like a nice guy. You weren't awkward with me or Emily at all. That means a lot to us. And because Corrie is one of our best friends, you'll probably be seeing us again. Treat her right, would ya? Otherwise you'll have to deal with *us*."

Corrie winced, but she should've known Quint would handle Bethany with grace.

"I like Corrie. Any friend of hers is gladly a friend of mine. I couldn't care less if you were male, female, tall, short, purple, or yellow. As long as you treat her as a friend should, I have no issues whatsoever. Good friends are hard to find. She, and I, would be stupid to care about all that other shit."

"Good answer." That was Emily. She hadn't said a lot, letting Bethany take the lead, but Corrie could tell she was impressed.

"And just so you know, I'd love if you guys could get together with me and Corrie and my friends sometime. I think you'd like Mackenzie and Mickie. They're girlfriends of two of my friends. You guys seem like the kind of people they'd like."

"Sure, that'd be great. Can't have too many friends. Thanks," Emily told Quint enthusiastically.

Corrie let go of Quint's hand and turned to Emily and held out her arms. She gave her a big hug, and then Emily passed her to Bethany. She repeated the gesture and then leaned down to kiss Ethan on the forehead.

"Good night, you guys. Drive safe. Emily, text me when you get home."

"Will do. You too, please."

"Of course."

"It was nice to meet you, Quint."

"You too."

Their goodbyes said, Emily and Bethany headed for their car. Corrie felt Quint once more take her hand in his and they walked to his car and climbed inside. He started it up without a word and pulled out into the night.

They'd been driving for a while before Corrie spoke up. "Thanks for tonight, Quint."

"For what?"

"For treating my friends like people. For not judging them. For being awesome. I think they really liked you."

"You don't have to thank me for that, Corrie. I was being honest with them when I said I didn't care about their sexual orientation. I've met a lot of horrible people in my line of work and it's what's inside someone that matters, not the superficial stuff. I can tell you're really close with them. I couldn't care less about any of that other societal crap." His voice changed from serious to teasing. "So are you dead set on getting home right this second? Or do you wanna do something fun?"

Corrie allowed him to change the subject. "I don't have any plans. I could use some fun."

"How about a driving lesson?"

"What? Quint! I can't drive!"

"Sure you can. I'll be right here to guide you."

"My seeing eye cop?"

He laughed. "Sure. That works."

"You're serious?"

"Yup."

Corrie was silent as Quint drove. Really? Drive? It was crazy. But if she admitted it to herself, it sounded like fun too. "If you won't get in trouble, I'd love to. Where are we going?"

"Someplace safe."

"I *hope* so," Corrie teased.

Corrie felt the car slow down about ten minutes later.

"Okay, we're here."

"Where's here?"

"The middle of nowhere." Quint laughed at the bewildered look that Corrie knew was on her face. "It's a random rural road. No one is out here. It's dark, the road is mostly straight. Come on, hop out and we'll change places."

Corrie got out, suddenly nervous. She couldn't believe he was crazy enough to let her drive his car. She kept her hand on the car as she made her way around the back. She ran into Quint and he grabbed her shoulders to keep her from falling. She looked up at him. "I'm not sure about this. You really won't get in trouble, will you?"

He kissed her hard. "It'll be fine. I won't get in trouble and I won't let anything happen to you. Trust me."

Corrie could only nod. He took her hand and led her the rest of the way to the driver's seat. He got her seated, fastened her seat belt, closed the door, and jogged around to the passenger's side.

"Okay, put your right foot on the brake pedal on the left."

Corrie did as he said.

"Good. Now hold on a sec." He adjusted something on the steering column. "Now, very slowly, ease your foot up off the brake."

Corrie did and felt the vehicle shift under her. She stomped her foot back on the brake and grunted as her seat belt kept her in place as she flew forward.

Quint didn't scold her, he merely laughed and told her, "Good. Do it again."

Corrie did as he instructed and felt the car move forward again. This time she kept her foot ready to brake again, but didn't immediately push it. "Holy crud, Quint. It's moving!"

"Yeah, sweetheart. You're driving."

"Not really."

"Okay then, let's drive. Keep your hands on the

wheel at the ten and two positions. For now, just keep your foot off the brake, don't push on the gas pedal to the right of the brake yet. I'll tell you to ease right or ease left on the steering wheel. Okay?"

Corrie nodded enthusiastically. "Okay. Yeah. Quint?"

"Yeah?"

"If I forget to tell you later…thank you. Most people treat me as if I'm totally helpless," Corrie told him breathlessly, loving that he was giving this to her.

She felt him lean into her and kiss her temple. "You're welcome. Just don't steer us into a ditch. I'm not sure I'd be able to explain it to the insurance company."

Corrie laughed and eased up on the brake pedal again. She smiled broadly as she followed Quint's directions.

He talked her through actually turning onto another street and then she got brave enough to even use the gas pedal. Heck, Corrie knew she wasn't going fast at all. Probably no faster than ten miles an hour, but it was exhilarating and exciting, and something she wouldn't have been able to do with just anyone. She trusted him not to let her steer the car into a ditch.

Finally, Corrie braked and turned to Quint with

what she knew was probably a goofy look on her face.

"Had enough?"

"Yeah, I think so. I'll never be Mario Andretti, but seriously, that was awesome, Quint."

He leaned over and moved the gear shift into park, explaining what it was to her this time. "You can take your foot off the brake now. It won't go anywhere. Come on, hop out and I'll get you home before your chariot turns back into a pumpkin."

Corrie giggled and undid her belt. She got out and started around the front of the car this time, keeping her hand on the metal to guide her. Once again, Quint met her halfway. This time he pulled her to him with a hand behind her neck. The other went around her waist and he drew her against him.

"You're beautiful." His words were whispered and reverent. Without giving her a chance to respond, he kissed her. It was a deep kiss, one that if they were anywhere but standing in the dark in the middle of a random rural road, would've led to more. As it was, it took a vehicle driving by and honking to bring them back to their surroundings.

Corrie realized she'd put both hands under his shirt and had been clawing at his back, trying to get closer. Quint's hands had also moved, one to her breast and the other to her ass.

Corrie put her head against his chest and laughed weakly. "We have to stop meeting like this." She loved the unrestrained snort that rumbled up through Quint's chest and out his mouth.

He didn't answer, but kissed her hard once more, and reluctantly pulled away. He grabbed her hand. "Come on, let's get you home."

They traveled back to her apartment in a comfortable silence. Quint pulled into a parking spot and asked Corrie to stay put. He came around to open her door and helped her out and, as usual, took hold of her hand and walked her to her apartment.

After she unlocked her door and entered the security code, she stood inside the door as he did a quick walk-through to make sure all was well. "All clear."

"Thanks for a good time tonight, Quint. I'm glad you like my friends, and I loved driving!"

"I've created a monster," he kidded her.

"You have no idea what being treated as if I'm not blind means to me. Most people wouldn't have even had the *thought* to let me do that tonight."

"I'll see what else I can come up with for you later. If there's something you've always wanted to do, or if there's something you want to experience, just let me know and I'll find a way to make it happen."

Corrie didn't answer, knowing her voice would probably break if she did. Instead, she stood on tiptoes to initiate a kiss and he cooperated by lowering his head and touching his lips to hers. He wouldn't let her deepen the kiss, and pulled back way too soon for her liking.

"I'd like nothing more than to make out in your front hall, then take you into your bedroom and get to know you even better, but it feels too soon."

Corrie nodded reluctantly, knowing he was right. She'd loved making out with him on her couch, and she'd loved giving him a massage, but that was then, this was now.

"Lock up behind me, sweetheart, and I'll talk to you later. We'll get together soon. Yeah?"

"Yeah. I'd like that."

"Don't forget to text Emily and let her know you got home all right."

Corrie's heart melted just a bit more. She would've forgotten if he hadn't reminded her. "Thanks for the reminder. I will."

He kissed her on her forehead and squeezed her hand one more time. "Good night, Corrie. See you soon."

"Night."

Corrie set her security system when the door shut behind Quint. She listened as he walked away from her door. She turned her back to the wall and put her hands around her stomach...and smiled a contended smile.

Things were looking good. Very good. She'd never been happier.

CHAPTER 10

CORRIE SMILED when her phone rang and the electronic voice told her it was Quint calling. It was about a month and a half after their first date, and they'd had a handful of other dates since then... including the date he'd let her drive. Corrie was realizing that Quint was about as perfect as she'd thought back on date one.

He certainly wasn't completely perfect...he swore too much and tended to be a bit too protective for her comfort level, but he was a generous tipper, liked her friends, and somehow seemed to understand her better than anyone ever had, other than maybe Emily and her parents.

Quint had also apparently been serious about learning Braille. Corrie had grappled with deciding if she wanted to start out with Braille 1 or Braille 2, finally deciding while it was more difficult, and not as widely used, having him start out by learning individual letters and numbers would help him more in the long run.

They'd sat at her table one night and started. Corrie had used her label maker to type out the alphabet. Braille wasn't easy to learn, even for a blind person. Quint was having a hard time, but Corrie was proud of his persistence.

"And here I thought English was a difficult language," he'd complained while struggling to be able to tell the difference between some of the letters.

"Close your eyes. I think it'll make it easier."

He had, and Corrie had put her fingers over his while he traced the dots. "Visualize what the dots look like on the page and memorize how they feel under your fingers. You'll have to move slowly at first, so you can understand what they say. If you move too quickly they'll all run together."

They must've sat at the table for three hours that first night while he'd attempted to get the basics down. The numbers seemed to be easy for him; he'd quickly picked those up, even was able to figure out simple math problems. He'd been so proud of himself and Corrie hadn't been able to resist giving him some positive reinforcement in the way of kisses every time he'd gotten an equation right.

They'd worked on his lessons here and there over the last three weeks, and while he'd probably never be fluent, and it was slow going, Corrie was impressed with his tenacity and his honest desire to learn.

Since she and Dr. Garza had reopened the clinic, they weren't getting the business they'd had before the shooting, but they were bouncing back...slowly. They'd had an open house, and invited the media, showing off their new security measures. They'd wanted to show the public they'd taken the extra steps to try to make sure something like what had happened before, would never happen again.

The media attention had, for the most part been successful, and Corrie was back to working every other day. She'd been reluctant to go back by herself at first, and Dr. Garza understood completely. They worked together for the first week they were back in business. Corrie would always be thankful to him for understanding her fears.

Shaun was still nowhere to be found and Dr. Garza had hired a new assistant for Corrie. Samantha was competent and Corrie liked her, but she still missed and worried about Shaun. No matter what horrible things he might have done, he'd been good to her and she missed him.

Not to mention, Corrie knew his wife was struggling. Robert's medical care was too much for her to deal with alone, never mind pay for. Her husband was missing and was a possible accomplice in a workplace shooting. Corrie felt horrible for her and their children.

Corrie closed her office door and answered her phone.

"Hello?"

"Hey, it's Quint."

"I know."

He didn't tease her like he usually did, but got right down to business. "Matt needs you to come down to the station today."

"Why?" Corrie whispered the word, not liking Quint's tone.

"I can't talk about it over the phone, sweetheart."

"I still have four patients to see today."

"I think that'll be all right. I'll talk to Matt. I can pick you up around three-thirty. Will that work?"

"Yeah, I think so. My last appointment is supposed to end at three. That'll give me time to record my notes before I leave." Corrie paused, biting her lip in consternation. "Is everything okay?"

Quint's voice dropped to the low, rumbly tone he used when he was trying to be gentle with her. It made Corrie's stomach clench. As much as she loved the sound, she hated knowing whatever he was going to say was going to be stressful.

"They found Shaun."

"Thank God! What'd he say? Where's he been? Did he explain everything that's been going on?"

"Sweetheart…"

It was the tone that clued her in. "Oh God."

"I'll pick you up at three-thirty. We'll talk then. In the meantime, be safe."

"I will. See you later, Quint."

"Bye."

"Bye." Corrie clicked off the phone and put her head on her desk. Crap. It was good they found Shaun, but she could tell by the seriousness of the conversation she'd had with Quint, whatever happened was bad. Crap crap crap. She'd wanted to ask a million other questions, but it was obvious Quint wasn't going to tell her anything sensitive or concerning over the phone.

She lifted her head, took a deep breath and got herself together. She had four more patients to see today, she had to give them her utmost attention. She didn't want to hurt them. The last thing the clinic needed was a lawsuit on top of everything else.

At three-twenty, Lori, their new administrative assistant, came to tell Corrie there was a gorgeous police officer in the lobby asking for her. Corrie smiled at her description. She might be blind, but she'd "seen" him in her many explorations, and would have to agree. Corrie hadn't been able to convince Quint she was ready to do more than explore each other from the waist up…yet. She'd been hoping tonight would be the night she'd finally get him out of his pants, but now with everything that was going on with Shaun, she wasn't so sure.

"Thanks, Lori. Tell him I'll be right out."

Corrie heard Lori leave her office and head back to the front of the clinic. She hurried to complete her notes on her last client and then pack up her stuff. She grabbed her cane, loving the fact that she only had to use it when she wasn't around Quint. She never felt the need to have it when she was with him because he always, every single time they'd been out, helped her get around by holding her hand. It'd become second nature to them both. Corrie felt more connected to him as a result. When she was holding his hand, she could pretend they were like every other couple on the street. She almost felt normal. Almost.

She headed out of her office and down the hall,

looking forward to being with Quint, no matter the circumstances. She opened the door to the waiting area and stopped, knowing Quint would come to her. Corrie felt a hand at her elbow.

"Hey, sweetheart. You look good."

Corrie smiled, knowing he was lying, but enjoying his words all the same. "Thanks, but I know better. I've been working all day and my hair is probably a mess and I can smell the medicinal lotion on my hands and clothes."

She felt Quint lean close and whisper in her ear as he ran a hand lightly over her hair. "You look delightfully mussed...it makes me wonder what you'll look like first thing in the morning. And I've grown addicted to whatever lotion you use while you work; one sniff and my body recognizes it as you...and reacts accordingly."

He moved slightly so she was flush against his side, and even with him wearing his utility belt with all his equipment, Corrie could feel what he meant. She blushed.

Quint chuckled. "Come on, sweetheart. Let's get this done. I have plans for tonight."

"You mean moving up to the next Braille primer?" she teased cheekily. Corrie loved the sound of his laughter.

"Yeah, that's what I meant," he drawled sarcastically.

Corrie waved goodbye to Lori and they headed out the door, her hand firmly grasped in Quint's as they headed for his patrol car.

"HE'S DEAD."

Corrie tried not to react, but knew she failed when she heard Quint growl from somewhere behind her. They'd arrived at the police station and had immediately been whisked into a room, where she'd been informed Detective Algood and another man called Conor Paxton had been waiting for them. Quint introduced everyone and he'd settled her into a chair at a small metal desk.

Detective Algood continued. "Conor is a game warden with Texas Parks and Wildlife, and was the one who received the tip about a body being found in Medina Lake. It's a miracle the body was even discovered; it looks like he was weighted down with plenty of cinderblocks, but he was dumped too close to shore. As you all know, we're way down in rainfall this year, and someone noticed something dark in the lake. When they investigated more, they saw a foot sticking up out of the water and called the Parks and Wildlife office. Conor went to check it out. Body's with Calder Stonewall in the medical examiner's office at the moment; it's unrecognizable, but it's looking pretty good that it's Shaun."

Corrie inhaled sharply. God, unrecognizable? She felt a comforting hand on her shoulder.

"Jesus, Matt. Remember who you're talking to," Quint groused.

"Sorry, ma'am. No offense."

"How can you know it's Shaun? I mean, if he'd been in the water that long…" Corrie asked tentatively.

"His clothes. His wife told us what she remembered him wearing the last time she saw him, and it matches perfectly."

"How did he die?"

Conor shared a look above Corrie's head with Quint. There was no way they'd want to share the horrible details with her. While the body had been decomposed beyond all recognition, it was missing its hands and there were several bullet holes throughout the body—nonlethal holes. One in the knee, one in each bicep, and two through the calves. The fatal bullet was the one in the middle of the man's forehead. It was obvious he'd been tortured before finally being executed.

159

"We're not sure yet, but Calder will figure it out," Conor said in a soothing, easy voice.

"So what does this mean?" Corrie couldn't understand why they'd felt it necessary to bring her in to tell her about Shaun.

Detective Algood spoke again. "It means whoever did this never wanted him found. If it wasn't for the drought in the area it would've been a very long time, if ever, before we found the body. It means you could be in danger."

"But I've been in danger since it happened, haven't I? So what's different now?"

Quint knew Corrie was smart. He wasn't happy she'd mostly figured it out so quickly, but he was impressed nevertheless. He knelt down by her side and put a finger under her chin and turned her face toward him. He hated seeing the worried look on her face.

"We assumed Shaun was probably dead, sweetheart. We also assumed the lack of any more threats against you meant they were backing off and leaving you alone. We're afraid since we found Shaun's body, and possibly clues, they'll once again turn their sights to you to try to make sure anything we *do* find can't be traced to them. The possibility of you being able to identify them is just another reason for them to be rattled...and pissed off."

Corrie tried to think through what Quint was telling her. "I still don't get it. If I can't testify, and didn't actually *see* anyone that night, why would they care about me?"

This was the part Quint had been holding back. "The district attorney hasn't ruled out you testifying."

Corrie inhaled sharply. "What? Really?"

"Yeah. With the shooting being on the national news, there's been a lot of attention focused on the department and the city. She wants to catch whoever did it, and after she heard everything you told Matt about how you could recognize the shooter, she's contemplating allowing your testimony."

"Oh my God. Quint…" Corrie reached out a hand. It landed on his chest and she slid it to his bicep. "That's great news! I wanted to testify from the very start. I know I can pick him out. I just know it."

Quint didn't even smile. He was pleased Corrie wasn't shying away from doing her duty and that she was eager to put the man behind bars who'd killed her friend and the others, but as the man, and cop, who was coming to care for her a great deal, he didn't like it one bit.

"I know you can too, sweetheart. And so do the

bad guys." He let that sink in. He knew it had when her forehead crinkled in concentration.

"Oh." She turned to the direction she'd last heard Detective Algood. "So now they'll want to shut me up too, won't they?"

Matt nodded, forgetting Corrie couldn't see him.

Conor answered her question. "Yeah, we think so."

Quint watched as Corrie literally pulled herself up by her bootstraps and blithely commented, "Okay then. I'll just have to be more careful."

He shook his head and half smiled. Jesus, she was cute, but totally clueless. He caught Conor's gaze and shook his head. Quint would break the news to Corrie.

Conor nodded at him and gave a head tilt to Matt, letting him know it was time to leave.

"I know you guys are talking without talking again," Corrie said peevishly, crossing her arms over her chest. Then, mumbling under her breath, continued, "I hate that."

Quint waited until the men had left the room. He pulled the chair sitting on the other side of the table around so it was next to hers. He physically turned the metal chair Corrie was sitting in, wincing as it screeched against the floor, until they were sitting face-to-face, knees touching. He picked up her hands and held them in his own.

"What is it, Quint? Tell me."

"I don't think you should stay at your place."

Panic crossed Corrie's face before she banked it.

"But I don't have anywhere to go. I already told you I won't stay with Emily and Bethany."

"What about your parents?" Quint knew what her answer would be, but asked anyway. He was purposefully leading her right where he wanted her.

"You know I won't do that either. Besides, they live up in Fort Worth. I can't leave Dr. Garza in a lurch like that. I can go to a hotel."

"There's no security in a hotel, Corrie. And what about all the other people there?"

"Crud. You're right. Darn it, Quint. What am I going to do?"

Bingo.

"Stay with me." Quint held his breath as Corrie absorbed his words.

"But...I don't..."

"I have a security system. I live in a house in a subdivision. If there are unknown cars in the area, my seventy-seven-year-old neighbor will let me know. She's a one-woman crime-stopper team." While Corrie bit her lip, Quint continued. "I have two extra bedrooms, sweetheart. I have lots of space.

I'm not saying I *want* you to stay in either of those bedrooms, but I'm not going to pressure you. You can stay with me and let me protect you. Once this is over, if you want, we can see where this chemistry between us goes. No pressure. Honestly."

"I don't do so good in unfamiliar places."

Quint sighed in relief. Her hesitancy wasn't because of him, but because of her nervousness about her lack of sight and his house. He took her hands in his and rubbed the backs of them with his thumbs as he spoke. "I know. You said as much when you told me Ian moved in with you rather than you going to his place. Sweetheart, I'm a bachelor. Have been for a long time. I don't have a lot of stuff. I'll walk you through my house as many times as you need to learn the layout. We'll bring over as much of your assistive things as you want. Hell, you can redo my kitchen however you need to. Trust me to take care of you, Corrie. I'm not that douchebag Ian. Trust that I'll make my home as comfortable for you as yours is. I swear I'll do whatever it takes."

"I'm not easy to live with."

"It'll be an adjustment for both of us."

"You have an extra bedroom?"

Quint's heart dropped, but he forced himself to say normally, "Yup."

"I want to stay with you."

"Thank God." Quint breathed the words. Not caring that they were in an interrogation room with a two-way mirror, he leaned forward, listening to his gear creak as he moved, and brought Corrie's mouth to his. He kissed her long and deep, putting the things he hadn't yet said into his kiss. He finally drew back and looked at her.

Corrie's hands were on his chest and she had a rosy glow on her face. Even with all that was happening, she was levelheaded and so gorgeous he almost couldn't believe she was here with him.

"On one hand, I hate this vest you're wearing because I can't feel *you*...but since I know you have it on to protect yourself, I can't *really* hate it."

Quint chuckled. Corrie constantly surprised him.

"Come on, sweetheart. Let's go tell Detective Algood where you'll be staying and we'll go to your place to gather your stuff."

"This doesn't mean you're getting out of your lesson today, buddy."

Quint pulled Corrie into his side and kissed her temple gently. "I didn't think it would." He shifted until he had her hand in his and headed for the door.

"Thank you, Quint."

He stopped. "For what?"

"For being you. For liking me as I am. For understanding I'm not like other women. For just...everything."

"You don't have to thank me for liking you and as far as you not being like other women...I thank my lucky stars every day for that. Come on. We have a lot of stuff to do tonight."

CHAPTER 11

CORRIE SAT NERVOUSLY on the couch in Quint's house. He'd been very patient with her as she'd decided what she needed to bring to his place, even going so far as to reassure her that if she realized she needed something she'd left behind, he'd be sure to collect it for her as soon as he could.

His house smelled good. Corrie didn't know what she'd expected it to smell like, but cinnamon wasn't it. He obviously had air fresheners strewn about to make it so fragrant, but Corrie wasn't complaining.

He'd held her hand and brought her straight to his sofa and told her to hang tight there while he brought in the rest of her things. She'd been all too ready to stay where he'd put her, because she didn't want to look like an idiot fumbling around his house trying to find her way. He'd said he'd show her around, and she was taking him at his word.

Corrie heard him go out to his garage a few times and walk down a hall into the back of the house. He'd puttered around in the kitchen a bit, most likely putting down the box of her kitchen doohickeys she'd decided she'd need immediately.

Finally she heard his footsteps coming closer to where she was in his family room. She felt the couch dip as he sat next to her and she sighed in relief when he took her hand.

"Relax, sweetheart. I promise you'll get through this."

"I'm just nervous. I don't like new places."

"I know you don't, but soon this will feel like your home too. I swear I'll do whatever you need in order to make you comfortable."

"I'm being silly, I know, I—"

Quint cut her off with a kiss. He pulled back and whispered against her lips, "You're not being silly. I'd feel the same way as you in your shoes. Just please, trust me to fix this for you."

Corrie took a deep breath. He was right. "Okay."

"Okay, first a tour. Then we'll decide where to put some of your things. Yeah?"

Corrie nodded and gripped Quint's hand tightly

when they stood up. "Lead on, oh brave warrior." She tried to lighten the mood.

Quint laughed as she hoped he would.

They spent the next hour touring his house several times. Quint never lost patience with her as he told her where his furniture was. He held her hand while they explored and she used her cane to gauge the distance between pieces of furniture and the width of halls and doorways. She felt more at ease after using it to figure out where things were and having Quint there to explain what everything was as she touched it.

After she'd been through every room twice, she began to feel comfortable enough to suggest moving some of the furniture here and there. She wouldn't have been so bold, but Quint had repeatedly told her it was fine and encouraged her until she made some suggestions. Of course he immediately agreed and they worked together to find the best layout of his stuff.

When they'd entered his bedroom for the first time, Corrie was extremely nervous, but Quint kept his tour clinical and she only caught a brief innuendo or two. He was trying to be on his best behavior.

Finally, after she'd walked through the house without holding onto his hand twice, and she was confident that she'd remember where she was and how it was all set out, she called it quits for the night. Corrie knew there'd be times she'd forget, she was too used to her own place, but she appreciated Quint's patience more than he'd ever know.

"How come you don't have a seeing eye dog?"

Corrie figured he'd ask at some point, since most people did, but she wasn't offended. "A dog is a lot of responsibility for someone who lives alone. I'm not opposed to one, heck, I love dogs, but knowing myself, I'd probably worry about its health, and what it was getting into that I couldn't see. For now, my cane gets me around just fine, and if I need help, I'm never afraid to ask people around me for assistance."

"Have you ever had one?"

"A dog? Unfortunately, no. My parents were allergic, and even once I moved out, I'd just gotten comfortable in my routine."

"You're off tomorrow, right?" Quint asked, changing the subject abruptly, as he was sometimes wont to do. It was as if once he got the answer he wanted, his brain was constantly in motion and he moved on to the next question.

Corrie smiled and did what she usually did, just went along with his change in conversation. "Yeah. It's Dr. Garza's day tomorrow."

"I've asked for the day off as well. We'll start on

the kitchen and you can tell me the best place for everything. We can try to set up the pantry and fridge the same way you've done it at your place."

"You're too good to be true, you know. Are you a cyborg? Something out of the future?"

Quint chuckled. "Nope. I'm just me."

"I like 'just you.'"

"I'm glad. I like you too."

Corrie knew she was smiling like an idiot, but couldn't seem to stop. "We're still going to hit the books tonight, though. I hope you know that."

Quint burst out with a short laugh. "Of course, slave driver. Let's do this." He pulled over the papers she'd printed out and concentrated on what she'd set up for him tonight. He reviewed the alphabet and only made a few mistakes.

"Okay, tonight we're going to start working on Grade 2 Braille. You ready?"

"Yup, sock it to me, woman."

Corrie shook her head and continued. "Okay, try this."

"I, L, Y."

"Right," Corrie praised, "but remember, this is Grade 2, the dots don't necessarily represent letters, but actually words.

"So the I might not be an I, it could be a word instead."

"Yup."

"How do I know the difference?"

"Most things nowadays are written in Grade 2, so it's a good bet if you come across something, it's actually a word and not the letter. You've got a short sentence in front of you in Grade 2. If I'd written it out in Grade 1 Braille, it'd be eight letters. But since it's in Grade 2, it's only three."

Corrie held her hand over Quint's as he traced the dots with his fingertips again. "What does it say?"

"I like you."

He traced the dots again. "Okay, so the I is really just an I. The L represents the word like, and the Y the word you. Cool. But I have a question."

Corrie could tell Quint was looking at her. His hand was motionless under hers.

"Shoot."

"How do I know the L represents the word like, and not loathe, or lick, or," he paused and his voice lowered seductively, "love?"

Corrie's heartrate jumped. "Practice, really. You have to figure out the context of what you're reading."

"Ummmm, so if *you* were sending me a letter in Braille it could be love, but if I got one from a scumbag prisoner, it would probably be loathe."

Corrie felt Quint put his free hand on her neck.

She knew he could feel her heart beating extremely fast. She nodded. "Yup, that's it."

"Got it." He paused and they sat there without saying a word for a moment. "I think study time is over. It's late. You have to be tired. Come to bed with me?"

He'd asked the question, but Corrie could tell he wasn't really asking if she was tired. It was finally time. She nodded enthusiastically.

Quint leaned toward Corrie and kissed her. He couldn't hold back. Jesus, having her here in his space, having her stuff all around his house, made it seem more like a home. He'd only brought one or two women to his house before, and it hadn't made him feel as comfortable as he was with Corrie here.

He couldn't wait to put her things away in his kitchen, to arrange it so it would work for her. Quint wanted to watch her making coffee in his kitchen. Wanted to see her cooking and being comfortable in her own skin in his space. He wanted her clothes hanging in his closet, her stuff on his bathroom counter and her sexy body in his bed, on his sheets. He had it bad.

He licked her lip as he pulled away and scooted back his chair suddenly. "Come on, sweetheart." Feeling like a bull in a china shop, he towed her quickly down the hall to his room, not bothering to turn off the lights as he went. Not wanting to let go of her, feeling as if he did, she'd disappear, Quint forced himself to drop her hand and turn her toward his bathroom.

"Go on, sweetheart. Bathroom is straight ahead, maybe five steps. Do what you need to do. I'll use the guest bathroom."

Corrie nodded and headed off to the bathroom, her arms held out in front of her cautiously so she didn't run into anything, as her cane was sitting on the kitchen table where she'd left it. Quint watched her backside sway as she headed for the bathroom and shook his head when she disappeared inside. He had to get himself together.

He quickly stripped off his clothes and carefully put them in the hamper in his closet. Usually he just threw them in the general direction of the plastic container, but he had a new reality now and couldn't afford to be careless anymore. He kept his boxers on and strode out of the room toward the guest bathroom to get ready for bed.

He got back to his room a few minutes later to see Corrie standing uncertainly by the edge of his bed. She had one hand on the mattress and was standing with her legs crossed, one foot on top of the other. He inhaled deeply at seeing her. She was wearing a long T-shirt, and he couldn't see anything else. He had no idea if she was naked underneath it or not, but her long legs about made his heart stop.

"Hey," she greeted nervously. "I didn't know which side you slept on."

Quint quickly came to Corrie's side and lifted her hand to his mouth. He kissed the palm and engulfed it in his own. "I don't really have a side. I'm usually in the middle."

She smiled at that. "Figures."

"Go on, climb in. Whatever side you're most comfortable in, you can have."

Quint almost groaned when Corrie lifted the comforter and scooted into the bed over to the far side, leaving room for him. He followed her in and gathered her close.

"Your heart is beating a hundred miles an hour. Are you that nervous? We don't have to do anything, sweetheart. We can just lie here. Sleeping with you in my arms is something I've dreamed about a lot over the last month."

Quint heard and felt Corrie sigh. "I am nervous, I can't deny it. But not for the reasons you may think."

"Just relax. You're fine."

"I know you probably have never thought about this, but you always smell so good. Your bed smells so good."

"My bed?"

"Yeah, your sheets smell clean, but it's mixed with you. The cologne you sometimes wear, the soap you use in your shower, the detergent you use…*you*. It smells like you."

"And that's a good thing?"

"Oh heck yeah." She paused, then continued, "I know I haven't seen you…there yet. And it's taking all my self-control not to push you over and rip off those boxers and examine the hard length I've been feeling against me every time we've made out."

Quint gurgled deep in his throat. It was a cross between a gasp and a laugh. "The feeling is definitely mutual, sweetheart. I don't know what you're wearing under that T-shirt, but my palms are actually itching to slowly ease it up your body until you're as naked as the day you were born. I know this is a he-man macho thing to say…but you have no idea what the sight of you on my sheets is doing to me. I've dreamed about it. I've even got myself off right here in this bed thinking about it. I think between the two of us, our first time is going to be pretty damn quick."

"Are you complaining?"

Quint could hear the smile in her voice. "Hell no."

"Did you turn off the lights?"

Quint took a moment to respond, not understanding her change of topic. "No."

"Good."

"Good?" Most women Quint had been with had asked him to turn the light off before they'd bared themselves to him.

"Yeah, I want you to have your fantasy. I can't wait to lie here naked, imaging your eyes on me. But I'll warn you, there'll be a time when I'll want the light off, simply so you can experience us together as I do."

"Jesus, Corrie. Every time you open your mouth I get harder."

"I can think of something *else* I can do with my mouth that will make you harder."

Quint couldn't think straight. He swore his vision went a bit gray at her words. He knew Corrie could speak her mind, and usually wasn't shy, but this...this was beyond his fondest fantasy. He'd always been annoyed when women hemmed and hawed about their looks. It wasn't as if he didn't understand, the media was murder on a woman's self-esteem, but maybe that was why Corrie was so self-assured and okay with her body. She couldn't see any of the pictures of the stick-thin women in Hollywood that were constantly on television, magazines and the Internet. It was refreshing as all get out to be with a woman who liked her body.

Quint grabbed the bottom of Corrie's T-shirt and

forcefully drew it up. He didn't ask, and she didn't protest. She merely lifted her arms to help him. He saw her dusky pink nipples briefly before leaning down to devour them.

He took one in his mouth and sucked hard, while his fingers found the other and tweaked it playfully. Corrie moaned in his arms and grabbed hold of his biceps while he played.

He wasn't nearly done when he felt one of her hands snake down his body between them. Quint helpfully pulled his hips away to give her room. She found his cock with no issues and squeezed him through the cotton of his boxers.

He lifted his head and gasped.

"God, Quint. You feel amazing."

"I think that's *my* line."

"We'll share it."

Quint tolerated her hand on him for another moment before rolling to his back and lifting his hips to remove the offending material. The sooner Corrie's hand was on his bare skin, the better. Before he could roll back over, Corrie was there. He looked up at her and grinned. She was so fucking sexy and she had no clue. No clue at all.

Her blonde hair was mussed and falling around her face. She brought one hand up and absently smoothed it behind one ear before putting her hand back on his body. Her cheeks were flushed and she alternated between licking her lips sensuously then biting the bottom one.

Her thighs were full, but muscular. He could see her quads flexing as she moved into place next to him. Quint knew they'd be soft under his hands.

Her breasts were perfect. They weren't small, but they weren't huge either. He could fit them in the palms of his hands easily. Her stomach was softly rounded and she had small love handles. Quint couldn't resist her, not that he had to hold himself back anymore. He'd seen glimpses of her before when they'd made out on her couch, but he'd never seen her like this. Naked, straddling his body, and all his.

He ran his hand over her breast and down to her stomach. Quint played with her belly button for a moment before moving his hand. He gripped her side, squeezing her skin until she shifted in his grasp.

"You are so soft. God, Corrie. You're amazing."

She didn't answer, but scooted back on his legs, breaking his hold on her and bringing her hands to his hips to explore. Quint drew in a quick breath as one hand cupped his balls and the other grasped his erection just under the head.

"You like that."

"Yeah."

Corrie didn't say more, simply continued running her hands over him. She learned his shape and texture. She used her fingertip to trace the head of his cock, smearing his pre-cum over him and massaging it into his skin.

Finally she spoke again. "Does it hurt?"

"Does what hurt?"

"This." She squeezed him lightly. "I can feel the veins sticking out and throbbing. It feels like it should hurt. Your balls are tight, I'm not sure I've ever felt anything like it before."

Quint didn't like being compared to anyone else, but ignored that for the time being. He ran his hand over her head, not offended in the least that she seemed to be staring off into the room. It didn't matter if her head was tilted down toward his cock or up at his face, she couldn't see him, at least not with her eyes. She was doing all the "seeing" she needed to with her hands at the moment, and it felt fucking awesome.

"It doesn't hurt…exactly. It's painful in a way because I'm so turned on, but it's a good hurt. I know that I'll soon be buried inside your hot, wet body and that it'll feel so damn good…it's worth any hurt I'm going through right now."

Without a word, Corrie leaned down and licked

the head of his dick. He groaned when she squeezed him and did it again.

Corrie's head came up and looked to where his face should be. "I want you."

Her words gave him the push he needed to take control. "Lay back." As good as her mouth felt against him, he knew he'd never last if he let her continue. There'd be time for that later...hopefully. If she wanted to.

She did as he asked and Quint pulled the sheet down until no part of her body was obstructed. He put one hand on her belly so she'd know he was there. He looked down at his tan hand against the pale skin of her stomach. It was so erotic, Quint knew if she touched him now, he'd explode.

As he looked at her, she stretched and arched her back. She put her hands up over her head and Quint swore she looked just like the pictures of Marilyn Monroe he used to drool over when he was young.

"Is it like you imagined?" Her voice was husky and sultry and slightly teasing.

"No." Quint clipped the word out without thinking. It wasn't until he saw Corrie frown and start to put her hands down that he realized what he'd said. He put his hands on her wrists and forced them back up over her head and leaned down to whisper in her ear. "It's so much fucking better, I'm about a second away from coming all over your pretty tits. Keep your hands there. Don't move. If you touch me, I'll lose it, and I have a lot I want to do before that happens."

The smile crept back over Corrie's face and Quint relaxed. He never in a million years wanted her to feel awkward in his bed...or anywhere for that matter. Quint eased down her body, licking here, nipping there, until he reached his final destination. He sat on his haunches between her legs. "Open wider for me, sweetheart." She did and Quint could feel his mouth watering. Oh fuck yeah.

Her folds were pink and glistening with her arousal. He eased down until he was on his belly between her legs. He put one hand under her ass and lifted her up. The other hand he used to spread her open for him.

"I hope you're comfortable, Corrie, because I have a feeling I'll be down here for a while." Quint smiled at the moan that escaped her mouth, but he didn't look away from his prize. He licked once, from bottom to top, paying attention to her clit when he reached the summit of her folds. As she jerked in his grasp he murmured more to himself than Corrie, "Oh yeah, a good long while."

CHAPTER 12

CORRIE HELD her breath as she felt Quint's tongue on her. Holy cripes, his touch was perfect. She desperately wanted to put her hands on his head, but she kept them where they were. She'd had a couple of men go down on her before, but it had been more of a "let's get this done so we can get to the good part" kind of thing.

But with Quint, he made *this* feel like the good part. He made it seem as if he truly was enjoying what he was doing. Corrie could hear his low moans and the sounds he made in the back of this throat. His grip on her butt was strong and every now and then his fingers flexed against her. She could feel his shoulders rub against her inner thighs as he concentrated on giving her pleasure. Corrie heard the sound of licking and the sound of her juices against his fingers as he used them to stroke inside her. It should've embarrassed her, but right now, it turned her on more.

Everything about what he was doing was hot as hell…and that was without being able to actually see it. She could only imagine what she looked like through Quint's eyes as he was up close and personal with her womanly bits. Corrie blushed, hoping Quint would be too busy to notice.

Quint loved Corrie's taste. If asked, he wouldn't be able to describe what she tasted like, but it was arousing as anything he'd ever experienced in his life. He moved his hips against the bed as he continued to lick and suck at Corrie's folds. He was so hard he knew the second he got inside her he'd lose all control.

He eased two fingers into her hot sheath and concentrated his attention on her clit. Quint could feel Corrie shaking as he pushed her closer and closer to the edge. He rubbed against her inner walls, trying to find her G-spot. When she jumped in his arms as he felt a small spongy spot inside her, he knew he'd found it.

"That's it, come for me, Corrie. Come all over my fingers. I want to feel it." He lowered his head and threw her over the edge with his dual assault on her bundles of nerves.

Quint struggled to keep his mouth on her clit as Corrie bucked in his hold. He smiled and his eyes stayed glued to her face as she thrashed in his arms. She moaned and he could feel her hands in his hair. He mentally smirked, realizing in the throes of passion she couldn't keep them above her head as he'd asked. Just as she was coming down, he used his fingers, which were still inside her, to stroke hard against the weeping walls of her sex one more time.

He lifted his head and watched as she shook uncontrollably in his arms once more. He'd seen other women come apart, but this was different. She wasn't moaning and carrying on. In fact, she wasn't really making much noise at all, other than a slight purr here and there. Her reactions to his ministrations were genuine and honest and somehow a hundred times sexier than anyone he'd ever been with. Corrie seemed to feel her orgasm from the tips of her toes to the top of her head. It was fucking awesome.

Quint pulled his fingers out of her body slowly, even as she continued to jerk and pump her hips into the air, appreciating how her body gripped him tightly, trying to prevent him from leaving her. He sucked his come-covered digits into his mouth, enjoying her strong musky taste. He pulled himself onto all fours and crawled up Corrie's body until he was hovering over her.

Her arms were lying limp at her sides and the cutest smile was on her lips. She looked completely sated and absolutely undone.

"Hey. You okay?"

"Shhhhhh."

Quint grinned. He didn't say anything, but leaned down and began kissing her neck. He nipped her collarbone and worked his way up to her ear. He took the lobe in his mouth and tongued it, then bit down gently.

Corrie moaned under him and finally moved her hands, bringing them up to his sides to grip him tightly. "Not fair," she mock complained even as she tilted her head to give him more access to her sensitive neck and ears.

"Don't mind me, sweetheart. Just lie there and ignore me."

"I couldn't ignore you if I tried."

Quint smiled again. She was so much fun. He'd never smiled this much while in bed with a woman before. In the past he'd been all about getting them off, then getting off himself. He'd never wanted to play and tease. He'd never known what he was missing.

"I want you, Corrie." Quint's words were serious

now. He pulled away and looked down into Corrie's face. She looked up. Her bright blue prosthetic eyes gazed where she calculated he was. Quint swore they could see right into his soul somehow.

"I want you too, Quint. I want to feel you inside me, filling me up."

"God." Quint gritted his teeth as his cock flexed against Corrie's stomach. He leaned over to the drawer next to his bed and pulled out the brand new box of condoms. He'd bought it last week in the hopes he'd get Corrie in his bed at some point. At the time he hadn't cared if that was months or days…although he was hoping for closer to the day timetable.

He tore at the box, cursing himself for not having the foresight to open it before now. In his rush to get it open, the condoms went flying everywhere as he jerked the cardboard top. Corrie threw her head back and laughed as she obviously felt the vinyl packets land on her body and around them.

She grabbed one that had alighted on her breast and held it up. "Looking for one of these?"

Quint leaned down and kissed Corrie hard and fast before taking the condom from her grasp. "Yeah, thanks."

He ripped open the foil, ignoring the other condoms now strewn over his bed, and leaned up on his knees to roll it down his eager cock. Quint inhaled as Corrie's hands knocked his away and finished the job.

Breathing through his arousal, he clenched his teeth and asked, "How'd you get so good at that?"

"Not how you might think," Corrie quipped as she pinched the tip of the condom and ever so slowly slid it down his cock.

"I didn't mean...sweet Jesus, woman...I meant..."

Quint's voice trailed off and Corrie answered what he was so badly trying to ask. "Hey, I might not be able to see, but I practiced right along with the rest of my health class in high school when it came to putting one of these babies on a banana."

"Did that really happen?"

"Yup. Can't imagine parents would allow it in the public schools today, but it was extremely enlightening for me and my friends. All done." She caressed his now-covered erection and tugged, encouraging him to finish what he'd started.

Trying to ignore how good her hands felt on him so he wouldn't go off before he'd even gotten inside her, Quint leaned back over her. "Hold on to my arms, sweetheart. This is gonna be hard and fast. I'm sorry. Next time I'll make it better for you."

"If this was any better, I'd be dead. I want you. I want to feel you inside me. Take me, Quint. Do it."

He waited until her hands gripped his upper arms before bracing himself on one hand by her head. Then he reached down and grabbed hold of the base of his dick with his other hand. He felt Corrie spread her legs even farther apart to give him room. He ran the head of his cock over her clit once, twice, then eased lower and pushed in. Quint groaned as he slowly drove himself into her hot, wet folds.

"Shit, Corrie. Jesus, you feel good."

Quint's hand came back up next to her shoulder on the bed to support himself as he pushed inside her warm body as far as he could go. He felt Corrie's knees bend and her legs wrap around his hips. She crossed her feet at the ankles and squeezed him. She tilted her hips and Quint swore he sank in another inch.

"God," Quint pulled out to the tip, then pushed in again slowly, "you feel," again he pulled out, then pushed in, "so fucking good."

Quint stopped talking; he couldn't get any other words out. His thrusts sped up as he powered in and out of Corrie. She felt like heaven.

"I can't…shit…hold on, sweetheart. Let me know if I'm hurting you…okay?"

Corrie groaned and pulled him closer. Quint fell onto his elbows over her.

"You're not hurting me. Do it. Please." Her voice was soft and breathy next to his ear. He felt her warm inhalations as she panted against his neck.

Quint let go of his restraint and pounded into Corrie as if his life depended on it. Amazingly, he felt her quake under him just as he lost control. He'd lasted longer than he thought he would…but only about two strokes longer. He held himself inside Corrie as he threw his head back and groaned.

Not able to hold himself up anymore, Quint eased down and to Corrie's side, making sure to keep one of her legs over his hip so his length stayed inside her for as long as possible. They lay there, both breathing hard, Corrie snuggled into his chest as Quint tried to catch his breath.

"Holy shit, woman."

Corrie giggled in his ear and Quint thought it was the most beautiful sound he'd ever heard.

They held each other for a few minutes, enjoying the aftermath of their orgasms. Finally, Quint pulled away reluctantly. "I have to take care of this condom, don't move."

Her leg eased off of him and Quint reached down and held on to the latex as he slipped out of her warm body, secretly loving the disappointed groan that came from Corrie's mouth. He leaned over, kissed her on the lips and whispered, "I'll be right back."

Corrie rolled to her back and smiled up in his general direction as she nodded. Quint went into the bathroom and took care of the condom. He turned on the water until it ran warm, and then wet a washcloth. He walked back into his bedroom and stopped, once more enjoying the sight of Corrie on his bed, naked. She'd turned on her side and was facing his direction. She had one arm under the pillow under her head, and the other was draped over her waist. Her legs were bent and she looked like a pinup model. Quint thanked his lucky stars she was all his.

He walked over to his bed and sat on the side. "Roll over on your back, sweetheart."

"Why?"

"I have a washcloth, I want to clean you up."

Corrie blushed and held out her hand. "I can do it."

"I want to." Quint held the wet towel out of her reach. "Please."

Without a word, Corrie rolled over, but kept her head turned toward the ceiling.

"You can't be embarrassed about this." Quint made small talk as he went about the extremely pleasant task of soothing her well-used folds and cleaning away the evidence of her arousal.

"I am."

Quint chuckled and finished what he was doing. "I enjoy it. I like making sure you're comfortable and have what you need."

She didn't say anything and Quint let it go. She'd get used to him. He hoped.

He didn't bother taking the washcloth back to the bathroom. He just dumped it on the floor by the bed, making a mental note to pick it up right when he got out of bed in the morning so Corrie didn't step on it. He couldn't imagine how gross it would be to step on a cold wet towel first thing in the morning.

Quint did his best to brush the condoms that had been scattered across the bed in their hurry off the mattress and then snuggled back into bed and pulled up the sheet, then the comforter. Something in his chest squeezed when Corrie didn't hesitate, but wrapped herself around him without a word. He felt her hand on his chest, tapping.

"What are you doing?"

"I'm writing in Braille with my fingertip."

Quint concentrated on what she was "writing." He smiled widely when he recognized the letters. He buried his face in her neck, crushing her fingers between them. "I like you too, sweetheart."

* * *

CORRIE ROLLED OVER AND GROANED. She was deliciously sore. It'd been a while since she'd had sex, and Quint wasn't a small man…anywhere.

She blinked—then stilled at the almost painful sensation. Crud. Every month she had to remove her prosthetics and give them a thorough cleaning. She hadn't done it this month yet, and with the pain she was feeling, it was obvious she'd put it off too long. She really didn't want to do it in front of Quint, but they were supposed to spend the day together getting his kitchen set up for her, so she wouldn't be able to avoid it. Her eyes really felt crusty and she knew it had to be done.

Corrie remembered when she'd put off the deep cleaning before. She'd gotten a terrible infection and had received a long lecture by her doctors. But she was embarrassed to take her eyes out in front of Quint. She'd once asked Emily what she looked like without them and her friend had been honest and told her it was a bit creepy looking. Emily had laughed and told her she looked like a character from a horror movie with the two blank holes where her eyes should've been. The last thing Corrie wanted was to look creepy in front of Quint, especially after the delicious night they'd had. They were still getting to know each other and she didn't want to look like a horror-show zombie in front of him.

Her prosthetics had to sit in the cleansing fluid for at least two hours, and really should be in there longer to give them the deep cleanse they needed. Shoot, Corrie knew she should've done it last night. They would've been done and ready to go by now if she had.

"What's wrong?" Quint's voice was sleepy by her ear.

"Nothing, go back to sleep." Corrie gave it a shot. She still felt Quint's head come off the pillow behind her where he'd been spooning her.

"I'm not tired. What's wrong? Are you having second thoughts about us?"

"No. Jeez, why do you have to be so observant?" Corrie complained a little petulantly.

"Because. Corrie, if it's not us, then what. Is. Wrong?"

He enunciated each word clearly. She could tell he was both irritated and worried by the tense way he held her in his arms.

It wasn't a big deal. Right? If she was going to be with him, she'd have to tell him sooner or later. "Ihavetocleanmyprosthetics."

"Okay…and?"

Darn. "And I have to take them out in order to do it."

"Yeah…" He drew the word out, beginning to sound confused as well as annoyed now.

Corrie turned in his arms and buried her face in his chest. He smelled so good, like him…and sex. It comforted her. "It's gross. I don't want you to see me without my eyes in."

She felt Quint pulling away. She sighed. She pulled back and looked up to where his face would be. She felt his hands on the side of her head, holding her still.

"You have to take them all the way out?"

"Uh-huh."

"Cool! Can I watch?"

Corrie drew back in confusion. "What?"

"I've never seen anything like it before. Does it hurt? How do you get them out? I didn't know they *came* out. I mean, of course they come out, they're prosthetics, but how do you clean them? Are they round?" He almost sounded like a little boy, excited for his first trip to see Santa or something.

Corrie reached up and blindly tried to find Quint's mouth. She missed at first, covering his chin, but readjusted her hand until it covered his mouth. She smiled at him weakly.

"I'll answer your questions if you really want to

know, but I want you to understand, without my prosthetics in, I'm weird-looking. Emily told me."

Quint moved her hand away from his mouth and leaned in until he could kiss both eyelids. "You'll never be weird-looking, Corrie. You're different. Yeah. So what? What we look like doesn't make us who we are inside. And you, sweetheart, are beautiful. You could have two heads and I'd still think so. I'm in like with you, and I'm quickly falling in love with you. Not with your eyes, or with your body, but with *you*. And this is a part of who you are. I want to know everything about you, this included. Okay?"

"Okay." It was the only thing she could think of to say. She wanted to screech like a little kid and bury her head into her pillow. He was falling in love with her? Holy crapola! She didn't have time to process it though, because Quint was herding her out of bed.

"Cool, let's go. I can't wait to see this."

Corrie just shook her head and followed Quint. He'd grabbed her hand and dragged her into his bathroom.

"Can I have a minute?" Corrie asked shyly.

"Shit, yeah, sorry. I'll go down the hall to use the other bathroom. Don't start without me."

Corrie laughed as she heard Quint hurrying out of the room and jogging down the hallway. She went back out into the bedroom and found her T-shirt that Quint had taken off the night before. Before they'd fallen asleep, Quint had sleepily leaned over, found it on the floor and told her he put it on the end of the bed so she could find it when she needed it in the morning.

Corrie went back into the bathroom and quickly took care of her morning routine and waited for Quint to return.

Quint breezed back into the bathroom and came up behind her. "Okay, carry on. I'm ready. Just pretend I'm not here."

Corrie shook her head and smiled nervously. As if. But she tried. She got out the supplies from her bathroom kit. She asked Quint for a clean towel and when he gave it to her, she covered up the sink in front of her. If she popped her eye out, she didn't want it to land in the hard sink and get chipped. She'd learned that the hard way too.

She pulled out the extractor from her cleaning kit and pulled her lower lid down until she could get the small edge of the plastic piece under the edge of the prosthetic. She pried it up until it cleared her lid and caught it in her other hand as it popped free of her eye socket.

The prosthetic wasn't round, as most people assumed. It was kinda oval shaped and hollow on the other side. It sat like a cup in her eye socket, rounding it out to make it look more like a normal eye.

Trying to ignore the fact Quint stood silently behind her, most likely watching everything she did with that observant way he had, Corrie continued with her cleaning ritual.

She used a wet cotton ball to clean away any dirt and discharge around her empty eye socket. Then she filled the eye bath with the special saline she made up at home and tipped her head back to wash out the socket of her eye.

Corrie then took the prosthetic and ran it under warm water in the sink, using the non-scented soap she carried with her to scrub it clean. She put it into a special container to let it soak in a bath of the saline solution. Some people didn't bother with this step, but she always felt it cleaned the eye better than simply running water and soap over it.

She put that eye to the side and started all over again with her other prosthetic. When she finished and both eyes were in the cleansing solution, Quint spoke for the first time. "How long do you soak them?"

"It depends. I usually keep them in the solution overnight, but today, two hours should do it."

Corrie felt Quint turning her in his arms. She

resisted for a moment but gave in. This was a part of who she was. He was right. If she wanted this to work, he had to see her without her prosthetics. She hated it, but it was better to do it now than later, when she was even more connected to him.

She felt Quint put his finger under her chin. Corrie lifted her head and waited, trying not to hyperventilate. She felt Quint's lips against her forehead, then her nose, then her lips, then she closed her eyes and felt him gently kiss both eyelids.

"You are beautiful, Corrie. Seriously. You are no less beautiful to me now, without your prosthetics, than you were lying naked on my bed waiting for me. And I have to say, and this is my inner geekiness coming out, that was the coolest thing I've seen in a long time."

Corrie snorted.

"Seriously. And sweetheart, I honestly don't see any difference in what you just did and what someone who wears contacts does every night. I don't want you to feel weird about that with me. If you need to take them out and clean them before we go to bed, do it. If you think that's gonna make me not want to bury myself deep inside your hot body, you're way wrong."

Corrie stumbled into him as Quint tugged her into his embrace. She could feel his cock, hard against her belly. "Having you here in my arms, in my bathroom, wearing nothing but that shirt, is almost as good as having you naked in my bed. Two hours, huh? Good. Plenty of time for me to make up for last night."

"Make up for it?"

"Yeah, I was a minuteman. I need to prove my virility to you so you don't think I'm always that quick."

Corrie giggled. "Don't we have stuff to do today?"

"Yeah, but it can wait. This is more important."

"Okay, I'm in. Show me what you can do." Corrie was more relieved than she'd ever be able to say. She'd been so afraid that he'd take one look at her empty eye sockets and be disgusted.

She laughed and grabbed hold of Quint's neck as he hoisted her up into his arms and headed out of the bathroom to his bed. Oh yeah, she was in like with this man. Definitely.

* * *

THE MAN USED his foot to crush out the cigarette he'd been smoking. So, the bitch had finally moved in with the pig cop. It made his plans harder, but not impossible. He'd finally learned the best way to get to her. It had taken two weeks, but he knew just how it'd go down now.

The boss was pissed the cops had already found Shaun's body. That wasn't supposed to happen. He'd been careful, but the fucking Texas heat had done him in. If there hadn't been a drought, no one would've ever found that fucker.

The man gritted his teeth when thinking about his boss. He was the most successful loan shark in the city, but he got that way because he was a complete asshole. He didn't trust anyone. He had no other staff...they'd all disappeared over the years.

The man wasn't stupid; he knew if he pissed the boss off, he'd disappear too, but for now the money was good and he enjoyed the side benefits of getting to kill and torture people and getting to screw whatever pussy he could get.

That thought brought him back to the present. He just had to wait a bit longer. The boss was securing a new place to take the blind bitch once she was grabbed. They had to figure out what she'd told the police and use her to set an example for others around the city who might be thinking about squealing about their business. The boss wasn't putting anything past her, though. They'd bring her somewhere she'd never be able to get away, and where her screams wouldn't be heard by anyone... and he'd get to have some fun.

The man reached down and adjusted his cock. He loved when he got to play with women. They were so much more fun to torture than men. When he shoved his cock up their pussy right off the bat, they usually cooperated much better.

The bitch was blind, which was weird, but he could work with it. No problem. She'd better enjoy fucking that cop while she could. Soon she'd be his to do with as he pleased. He couldn't wait.

CHAPTER 13

CORRIE LAY in bed and listened to Quint get ready for work. He had an early shift and she was more than happy to go back to sleep for a couple of hours. They'd been up late the night before because they couldn't keep their hands off each other. The last time they'd made love, Quint had kept his eyes closed the entire time at her request. He'd told her it was the most intense experience he'd ever had. Corrie smiled at the memory.

He'd started by caressing her from her head to her feet, and then after he'd teased her unmercifully until her toes curled, Corrie pushed him to his back and returned the favor. She'd enjoyed his moans and groans as she'd run her hands and lips all over his body. She'd taken him deep within her mouth and Quint had told her how incredible, how much…*more*…it had felt like when he could only imagine what she was doing and couldn't watch.

He'd pulled her off his cock before he'd exploded and turned her over. He'd urged her to her hands and knees and had taken her from behind. After rolling on a condom, Quint had powered in and out of her with a slow and steady rhythm, keeping up a running conversation about how good she felt, how soft she was, how he loved feeling her skin ripple and shake under his hands. He'd even smacked her ass lightly and marveled at the feel of her ass heating up under his ministrations.

It finally took Corrie snaking a hand under them and caressing his balls as he slowly entered her to get him to lose his iron control. He'd taken hold of her hips in his hands and had slammed himself inside her. Corrie had lost her balance and fell to her forearms on the bed, but the change in angle simply seemed to make him lose even more of his control. They'd both moaned and groaned until first Corrie, then Quint, had exploded.

He had eased himself down to the bed and held Corrie to him and they'd lain there without words for what seemed like forever. Finally, Quint had eased out of her and headed to the bathroom to dispose of the condom. He'd returned with a warm washcloth, as he always did, and after cleaning them both up, he'd snuggled in behind her again and whispered all sorts of amazing things while kissing her neck and shoulder.

It had been incredible...but then again, each time Quint made love to her, it was mind-blowing.

It'd been seven days since Corrie had essentially moved in with Quint, and he'd kept his promise and done everything possible to make her comfortable in his home. She'd been extremely worried about it, but so far it was working out.

Corrie knew she was moving way quicker with Quint than she probably should, but she couldn't help it. He worked hard, was attentive to her without being smothering, was loyal to his friends to a fault, was romantic, and the chemistry between them was off the charts.

As she'd noticed before, Quint wasn't perfect. He had a habit of throwing f-bombs around a little too much and sometimes when he slept on his back he'd snore loud enough to wake the dead. She also had a feeling he still tended to think of her as fragile because of her blindness...but for now, their relationship was working well. She'd have plenty of time to work on that other stuff with him. She hoped.

She listened as the shower turned off and Quint wandered around the room getting dressed. There was something very intimate about listening to him put on his clothes. Corrie never would've guessed. She hadn't felt this way about Ian, not even close.

Corrie heard the creaking of Quint's equipment belt as he walked toward her, and felt the bed dip as he sat down next to her hip.

"You gonna sleep for a while?"

"Um-hum."

"Okay. You have to be at the clinic at nine?"

"Yeah, my first appointment isn't until nine-thirty so I get to go in a bit later today."

"Emily is picking you up?"

They'd argued about this the night before as well. Quint had been taking her to work every day, but since he had to go in so early, she didn't want to inconvenience him by having him come back to the house during his shift. She was also being selfish by wanting to sleep in, and not get to work as early as she would if he took her in when his shift started. Emily had never minded picking her up, and when she'd asked, her friend had agreed immediately. It'd been a while since she'd had her Emily fix and they were both looking forward to catching up.

Corrie knew she had to think about rescheduling the car service she'd been using before everything had happened. She'd temporarily canceled it after the shooting, but she hated always relying on Emily and Bethany, and now Quint, to take her everywhere she wanted to go.

Realizing Quint was waiting for her answer to his question, she quickly said, "Yes, she'll be here around eight-thirty. We'll talk a bit, catch up, then we'll go. It's fine."

"Okay. Want to have lunch together?"

Corrie mock frowned up toward Quint. "You've taken off for lunch every day of the last week. Aren't you going to get in trouble?"

She felt his hand smooth over her head and tuck her hair behind her ear. "No. We *are* allowed to eat while on shift you know."

"Okay then, yes. I'd love to have lunch. I'd never turn down spending time with you."

Quint leaned into her and brushed his lips over Corrie's forehead. "As much as I'd rather crawl back into bed with you, I gotta get going."

Corrie brought her hand up to the back of Quint's neck and pulled him down to her mouth. She kissed him long and hard before pulling back. "Okay, go on then. I'll see you later."

"Jesus, sweetheart. Now I have to go to work with a hard-on."

Corrie giggled. "You'll live. Now go. I'll see you at lunch."

"Maybe if I play my cards right I can get a

lunchtime quickie," he teased playfully. He kissed her one more time quickly and backed away. "I'll set the alarm and lock up as I leave. Stay in bed, enjoy your lazy morning."

"Okay, thanks."

"Bye, sweetheart. See you later."

"Bye, Quint."

Corrie smiled and snuggled deeper into bed as she listened to Quint walk through the house, fiddle around in the kitchen, and walk out the door. God, she loved him.

Wait. What?

Corrie thought about it. Yup. It hadn't been that long, but she could admit it, to herself at least. She loved him.

He'd shown her in a million ways how much she meant to him...from putting all his clothes in the guest-room closet—and then arranging all her stuff in the master closet so it was exactly as it had been at her own house—to putting some of his furniture in storage so there would be more room to walk around and less chance of her hurting herself.

They'd also painstakingly rearranged the kitchen together, making sure she could reach all the plates and cups and cooking utensils. He'd added a shelf to one of the cabinets so all of her cooking spices could go there in the same order they'd been in at her own apartment.

And not once—not one single time—had she tripped over something he'd accidentally left out. He was super conscientious about putting his things away. Everything had its place, and so far he'd stuck to it. Corrie knew it couldn't last forever; it was inevitable that he'd forget something, but with as much effort as he'd been putting into trying to make sure he didn't leave anything out of place, Corrie knew it would devastate him when it did eventually happen.

Quint was attentive to all her needs in bed, he was sexy as all get out, and he was trying so hard to learn Braille, it almost made her heart hurt. Even her parents hadn't tried this hard to be able to read and write the way she did. They'd made a halfhearted attempt when she was younger, but with the escalation of technology, and the ability for her to "read" the computer and emails, they'd given up.

Corrie thought back to the day before when Quint had shyly handed her a note he'd meticulously used her Braille label maker to write. It was awkward, and he'd mixed both Grade 1 and 2 Braille, but she was able to read it. It'd said: *You make me happy. The luckiest day of my life was when you ran into that busboy.*

It was the first time she'd cried in front of him, and Corrie thought he was going to lose it. He'd been horrified that he'd made her cry, until she went down to her knees and had taken him in her mouth as a thank you.

She grinned at the memory. God, she loved how he smelled…and tasted. Corrie turned on her side and pushed a button on her specialty clock.

Alarm set for seven-thirty, the monotone computerized voice said.

Corrie snuggled back down into the blankets, satisfied that she had another hour and a half to sleep. She fell asleep immediately, dreaming of Quint.

* * *

CORRIE WOKE UP WITH A START. Someone was ringing the doorbell to Quint's house. The loud *ding-dong* echoed around the room, then faded. She reached over and pushed the button on the clock.

Seven-thirteen a.m., the mechanized voice announced.

Corrie threw her legs over the side of the bed and reached for her T-shirt as the doorbell pealed again. She threw the shirt over her head and hurried to the closet. She went to the shelf and felt for her sweatpants. She didn't bother looking for the Braille tag that would tell her what color they were, but simply pulled the first pair she touched up her legs. She kneeled down and felt for her shoes, and grabbed the pair of flip-flops that was on the end of the row.

"Coming!" Corrie called out as the doorbell rang again. Maybe Emily was early. It wasn't like her to be early for anything though. Typically she was right on time. Corrie had made fun of her more times than she could remember for having an annoying habit of being right where she was supposed to be at the exact time she was supposed to be there.

Corrie stopped at the front door. "Who is it?" she remembered to ask before simply opening the door.

"It's Bethany."

Corrie frowned. What the hell was Bethany doing there?

Oh Lord—Emily or Ethan. Something had to be wrong!

Corrie turned to the alarm panel next to the front door and punched in the numbers to disarm it. She unlocked and opened the door. "Bethany? Where's Emily? And Ethan? Are they okay?"

Corrie heard Bethany whisper, "I'm so sorry," before the strike to her head rendered her unconscious.

* * *

QUINT SAT across the desk from his friend Calder Stonewall, the medical examiner who'd been responsible for the autopsy on Shaun's body. San Antonio wasn't a huge city and they'd crossed paths so much in the past, they'd become close. They had a law enforcement clique of sorts, with five others in various law enforcement agencies.

"Talk to me, Calder. What sort of sick fuck are we dealing with?"

"You're not going to like it, Quint."

"I know I'm not. Sock it to me."

"I don't have the hands to be able to tell, but based on the fact that each of his toes were cut off, I'd bet they did the same to his fingers before cutting off his hands altogether."

"Christ. Go on."

"Lots of typical shit. Cigarette burns, broken ribs, bruises, and petechial hemorrhaging."

"They strangled him?"

"Probably repeatedly. They most likely cut off his air until he passed out, then waited until he wasn't unconscious anymore to do it again."

"Fuck."

"What did they want, Quint? This isn't normal shit. This is highly sadistic behavior and not the sort of thing criminals around here are usually into. If the man didn't have any money, what would torturing him do? It's unlikely he was hiding money from them, he was legitimately broke. Whoever did this is unstable and *enjoys* what he's doing, and does it extremely well. I'd expect to see this sort of thing with the mob or something, not here in San Antonio."

"Detective Algood wasn't able to find out a lot, but after we called in Cruz and the FBI, they were able to piece together some of what Shaun had gotten himself into."

Calder nodded for Quint to continue.

"Since Shaun's son had his accident, they were hemorrhaging money. It costs a fuck of a lot of money to keep that kid alive. First the hospital bills on the day of the accident, then the medical bills to keep him alive and functioning. Catheters, breathing machines, feeding tubes, mechanical beds, prescriptions, round-the-clock medical care…you name it, that kid needs it. There's no way a normal family can afford all that shit."

"He made a deal with the devil then?" Calder asked.

"Yup. Specifically, a Mr. Dimitri Prandini."

"Holy shit, he had a death wish, didn't he?"

"I'm assuming he had no idea what he was

getting into." Quint and Calder both knew Dimitri because he was a local loan shark…one who wasn't known for his touchy-feely ways. "Apparently he borrowed more than a hundred thousand dollars and when Dimitri wanted to collect, with interest, Shaun couldn't pay. He sent his henchman, Isaac Sampson, after him to collect."

"How does a man with only one employee get to be such a success?"

Quint grimaced and nodded in agreement. "I know. By all accounts, the other sharks around here should've gobbled him up by now. But Dimitri is especially vicious. I heard from Cruz, the FBI has been keeping their eye on him, and would love to arrest him, but they don't have enough hard evidence yet. When he first started in the business he had about a dozen 'helpers.' They'd troll the city looking for schmucks who were stupid enough to gamble away money they didn't have. Dimitri also ordered hits on the other loan sharks for no fucking reason. His henchmen would just ambush them and kill them outright."

"But, Quint, that doesn't make any sense. Didn't the other sharks band together against him or something?"

"Yeah," Quint agreed grimly. "They did. And

Dimitri changed tactics from ambushing the sharks, to ambushing their women."

"Jesus."

"Yeah, Dimitri has no soul. None. He ordered his men to kidnap, rape and torture the wives and girl-friends of anyone who publically spoke out against him. There were still some rumblings of the sharks ganging up and putting an end to Dimitri's reign once and for all, until he went after an entire family."

Calder didn't say anything, just growled.

"Needless to say, it wasn't pretty. The man had three daughters…ages three to twelve. Dimitri's thugs started with the oldest daughter and worked their way down. Then they started on his wife, and finally killed the guy. After that, no one has dared to go against him."

"And his posse of henchmen?"

"No one knows for sure, but rumor has it Dimitri's paranoid and decided one day that they were all out to get him, and he disposed of them all."

"Jesus fucking Christ. And this guy ordered the hit on Shaun at the chiropractor office?"

"Yeah."

"And he's now gunning for your woman."

Quint hadn't told any of his friends how serious he was about Corrie, but apparently he didn't have to. It was obvious enough. "Yeah."

"But how does your Corrie fit into all this?"

Quint couldn't deny the words "your Corrie" settled right into his soul as if they belonged there. "They're trying to tie up loose ends. Dimitri isn't the smartest tool in the shed, and Isaac isn't much better. He's the last of his henchmen, and known to be the most sadistic. I'm assuming they think if they can get to Corrie and shut her up, they'll get away with the murder of both Shaun and all those people from her clinic, scot-free."

"Dumbasses."

"Yeah."

Before Quint could say anything else, the phone on his desk rang. He leaned over and picked it up.

"Axton here. What? Yeah, she knew. She was planning on getting there around nine. Are you sure? Okay, I'll give her a call. She might have over-slept. Thanks, Dr. Garza."

Quint hung up the phone and swore.

"Everything all right?" Calder had picked up on the urgency in Quint's tone.

"Not sure. That was Corrie's partner. She was supposed to be at work at nine, but Dr. Garza just heard from Lori, their new admin, and she hasn't shown up yet." Quint looked at his watch. Nine forty-five.

He dialed Corrie's number and waited. She didn't

pick up. He dialed it again, and once again it went to voice mail after four rings. The hair on the back of his neck stood straight up and goose bumps sprung up all over his arms. "Fuck. Calder, I gotta go. Let me know if you find anything else out."

"Want me to call Cruz and the others?"

Quint didn't hesitate. "Yes. Something's wrong. I feel it."

"On it. Go."

Quint didn't wait, thankful he could rely on Calder to get him some backup. He strode from his desk straight to his deputy chief's office. He had to get SAPD rolling. He didn't have an extra second to spare. Corrie might not have that extra second. He had a bad fucking feeling about this, and it didn't help that he'd just recounted what horrible human beings Isaac and Dimitri were. Calder's description of what Shaun had gone through raced through his mind on repeat.

Fucking hell.

Quint raced through his neighborhood with his lights and sirens blaring. He didn't know how he knew this was bad, he just did. Two other patrol cars followed behind him with their lights on, but no sirens. Cruz was meeting them at his house as soon as he could get there.

All looked quiet at the house as Quint screeched

to a halt, skidding up onto his lawn as he fought to control his car. Without bothering to take the keys with him, although he did flip off the siren, Quint crouched and ran, gun drawn, toward his front door.

The door was closed—but Quint could hear the screaming of an infant clearly though the thick oak.

What the holy fuck?

He noticed with detachment that his hands were shaking as he pulled out his house keys and put them in the lock. It was stealthier to open the door with the keys than to kick it in. And if anyone was in the house, he didn't want to give them a head's up he was inside.

The door swung open and Quint looked at the alarm panel.

Off. *Fuck.*

The wail of the baby crying was louder now that they were inside the house. The infant was clearly in distress. It wasn't a "give me food, I'm hungry" cry, it was a "if I don't get attention immediately, I might die," kind of screaming.

As they'd been trained, the officers ignored the distressed cries coming from the back of the house as they concentrated on making sure the area was safe. In an active-shooter scenario, the scene had to be cleared before any wounded victims could be taken care of. It was one of the hardest things to have to do…ignoring the pleading and cries from any injured persons begging for help, and to step over them, if necessary, to make sure the scene was safe for the first responders and the rest of the potential victims.

Quint gestured one officer to the right and the other to the left, to take his back. They methodically went through the kitchen and the living room. Both were empty. The baby's screams were coming from down the hall. They cleared both guestrooms and the bathroom.

The last room was the master bedroom.

The door was shut. Quint put his hand on the knob and looked to both the officers. They nodded at him, indicating they were ready, and he twisted the door handle and brought his hand back up to his pistol. Quint had no idea what they'd find, but he prayed harder than he ever had in his life that it wouldn't be Corrie, bleeding and possibly dead.

They surged into the room—and Quint's stomach dropped to his toes.

Jesus fucking Christ.

Bethany was on his bed.

He was surprised to see Corrie's friend, and not Corrie, but it was how they found her that really shook him to his very soul. She'd been crucified to the wooden headboard with a knife through each of her palms.

She was conscious, which greatly relieved Quint, but she was obviously in a lot of pain and moving with agitation on the bed.

Ignoring the woman for the moment, the three officers continued to clear the room. It was empty, with no sign of Corrie, Emily, or any bad guys. Quint headed to the bathroom, not stopping to reassure Bethany as she pleaded with him to help her son.

Inside the bathroom, Quint immediately saw that Ethan's life was in extreme danger. He was on his back in the bathtub. The stopper had been put in the bottom and the water had been turned on. It wasn't dripping, but it wasn't gushing either. It was a sluggish stream that was slowly filling up the tub, with Ethan in it, helpless on his back.

The baby was naked and screaming. His face was bright red and he was flailing his arms wildly. The water had filled the tub enough that most of Ethan's body was under it. The water was halfway up his chest and quickly getting higher and higher. If they'd been even an hour later—hell, thirty minutes—the water would've covered his face completely and Ethan would've drowned.

Quint holstered his gun without thought and

reached for the frightened baby. The water was ice cold. No wonder Ethan was screaming. He grabbed a towel off the rack and swaddled the infant up as best he could before cradling him against his chest and rubbing his back soothingly. Frigid water dripped from the wet towel onto Quint's shirt and the vest underneath, but he didn't even feel it.

Quint heard the second officer calling for an ambulance and the crime scene techs. He turned back into the bedroom. Ethan was still crying, but it had changed from a terrified wail, to more hiccupping sobs. He'd burrowed into Quint's chest and lay against him, almost unmoving, except for his little chest heaving with his sobs.

Quint walked over to his bed where Bethany lay, tears streaming down her own face. He could tell she'd struggled, but she hadn't been able to stomach the pain it would have taken to release herself from the knives through her palms.

"He's okay, Bethany. He's fine. Cold, but fine." He watched as she tried to control her crying. "The ambulance is on the way, you're both going to be just fine. I swear. Can you tell me what the fuck is going on? Where's Corrie? Where's Emily? What happened here?"

"A guy showed up at the house this morning." Bethany's voice was agonized. "He broke in and grabbed Emily. He told me he'd kill her if I didn't do exactly what he told me to. He looked crazy. I believed him."

Quint nodded and urged her to continue.

She spoke through her sobs, understanding how important it was to get as much information to Quint as possible. "He told me to hold Ethan, then he tied Em up and beat the ever-loving shit out of her. He told us we were dykes and not fit to walk around on the planet. He said if I tried to stop him, he'd kill Emily with a bullet in her brain right there in front of me. That if I got away, he'd rape and then kill her. She looked at me as he was beating her, with pleading eyes. I knew she was begging me to take care of Ethan and not worry about her."

"Bethany, I know you're in pain, and help is coming, but I need you to tell me your address so we can get help for Emily," Quint ordered as gently as he could.

Quint turned to the officer standing behind him, looking on helplessly. They both knew if they tried to take the knives out of Bethany's palms, it could kill her. She'd already lost too much blood. Her face was deathly pale. He really didn't have to tell the officer, but immediately after Bethany whispered her address in a pained voice, he ordered, "Call it in."

The officer nodded and turned away, already

keying his mic. Quint heard him telling dispatch about the other woman. They'd get units to Emily's house and make sure she was okay.

Quint turned back to Bethany. Corrie was his concern now. He kept rocking Ethan and rubbing his back, trying to calm him down. "We've got officers headed to your house to check on Emily. Please, what happened here? Where's Corrie?"

"After he beat Em into unconsciousness, he forced me into his car. I wanted to leave Ethan at the house, but he grabbed him from me. He drove here with Ethan on his lap, ranting the entire time about how he was an evil child, that Ethan would be better off if he just killed him now instead of letting him grow up as the son of a lesbian couple. I wanted to do something, but I didn't know what. I thought about bailing out of the car, but that'd leave him with Ethan. I couldn't leave my baby. He would've killed him on the spot."

"Shhhh, I know you couldn't. You did the right thing. Then what?" Quint tried not to lose his patience, just put a soothing hand on her leg.

"He held a knife to Ethan's throat and forced me to knock on your door. Corrie answered and I told her it was me. She opened the door and he hit her hard enough to knock her out."

Quint saw red and squeezed the baby a bit too

hard. Ethan cried out, but settled again when Quint bounced him in his arms soothingly.

Bethany continued, her voice growing weaker. "He left her on the floor and forced me in here. He threw me on the bed and pulled the knives out. He told me I had a choice…either I lay still and let him do…this, or he could do it to Ethan." Bethany gasped and Quint saw the tears fall from her eyes again.

"He swore he'd put him on the floor and leave him alone if I did it. So I lay still and let him stab me. I never knew anything could hurt so damn bad. As I lay there screaming, he took Ethan into the bath-room, telling me all the while what he was doing and how Ethan was going to die anyway. I yelled at him to leave him alone, that he promised, and he only laughed at me. Then he left. I tried to get up but I couldn't. It hurts, Quint. It hurts so damn bad."

Quint moved his hand from her leg to her fore-head to try to console her. It was a safe place he felt he could touch and not hurt her further. "Did he tell you where he was going? Anything that will help us find Corrie?"

"No."

"*Think*, Bethany. Anything you can remember, even if it seems as if it's nothing, will help us at this point."

Quint held his breath as Bethany closed her eyes

and thought back through what had happened that morning.

Her eyes opened and Quint could see her mentally straighten her shoulders. He'd never been so relieved. She looked up at Quint. "He mumbled something while we were driving through rush-hour traffic about how he hated the city and couldn't wait to get out to the cabin."

Quint closed his eyes briefly in thanks. Bingo. It had to be enough. It was a long shot, but knowing they were in a cabin outside the city was more than they would've had to go on without Bethany. He leaned over her and kissed her forehead, much as he did with Corrie when he was trying to comfort her. "Thank you." Quint could hear the ambulance arrive and the EMTs enter his house. "You're going to be fine. Ethan's okay, and they'll get to Emily as well."

Her eyes stared up at him, glassy with pain, but clear. She was one tough chick. Quint was glad Corrie had her as a friend. "You'll find her? You'll keep that asshole from hurting Corrie?"

"I'm going to do my damnedest."

Bethany nodded and the medical personnel came into the room. Quint handed Ethan off to one of the men, leaving the explanations about what had happened to the other officers. They'd been standing behind him when Bethany told him what happened.

Quint stepped into his living room to find Cruz there, along with Dax, their friend TJ, and even Hayden Yates. TJ was a Highway Patrolman, but he'd never shied away from helping wherever he was needed. He'd been there when Dax had confronted the serial killer who had buried Mackenzie alive. Hayden was a sheriff's deputy, and she was one of the toughest law enforcement officers Quint had ever met, male or female. He'd take all the help he could get right now.

He quickly explained what Bethany told him had gone down that morning.

"So she's been gone about three and a half hours now," Cruz calculated. "Do you think she has her cell on her?"

Quint looked over to see Corrie's purse on a hook by the front hall table. He strode over to it and held his breath. He reached into the small pocket and pulled out her phone where she always kept it and showed it to the others. Damn.

"Okay, so we can't use that to track her. What else we got?"

"Cruz, who do you know that can dig deep and find us information?" Quint asked, desperate.

He shrugged. "The guys at the bureau are good, but are somewhat limited because of…you know….laws."

"Fuck." Quint spat out the word. "This all needs to be on the up and up so it doesn't get fucked up. I know this is Dimitri and Isaac. It's the only thing that makes sense. But going through proper channels is going to take too long."

"I might know someone," TJ said quietly.

Four sets of eyes swung to the Highway Patrolman. He spoke before anyone could ask. "You guys all know I used to be Delta Force. There were times we relied on an outside guy to get us some intel on our marks or to give us some extra recon before we went on missions. He's totally legit…works for the government, but I'm fairly certain how he gets his information isn't always completely legal."

"Call him," Quint said immediately. He didn't care how the man got his information, as long as it led them to Corrie.

"If he comes through, we'll need a cover story on how we found her," TJ warned.

Quint looked around at the best friends he'd ever had. The only two missing were Conor and Calder. "If it was Mackenzie, would you do it?" he asked Daxton.

"In a heartbeat," was his immediate response.

"Please, TJ, call your guy. I'll take the rap for this if it comes to it. Corrie means more to me than anything, even my job."

TJ didn't say another word to try to dissuade his friend; he clicked on a contact in his phone and put the phone up to his ear. After only a moment, he began speaking to whomever it was who answered. "Ghost. It's Rock. Yeah, I know, it's been too long. I need Tex. Yeah, C-Red." He held his hand over the speaker and interpreted for his friends, "Code-Red." His attention was brought back to the phone as the mysterious Ghost continued to ask questions. "We need intel immediately. Kidnapped. Thanks, I appreciate it. We totally need to get together soon. I heard you snagged yourself a woman." He chuckled at something the man on the other end of the phone said, then got serious again. "Thanks, I appreciate it. I'll let you know how it goes. Later." TJ clicked off the phone.

"Well?" Quint asked impatiently.

"Give him a moment. He'll call. Ghost is going to get a hold of him."

"Why don't you have this guy's direct number?" Hayden asked.

"Tex is…eccentric. He knows everyone, and those of us who have worked with him understand that while he can find us at a moment's notice, he doesn't want his contact information spread across all the groups and men he works with. Only the team leaders have his direct line, and even that changes almost monthly. Look, the man could disappear with his family and no one would ever find him, he's that good. He makes himself and his computer abilities available to us in emergencies."

"What does he want in return?"

"A marker. He'd never take money for anything he does. He claims the government pays him more than enough for him and his family to live on. But he lives and breathes information. If he needs us, he'll let us know."

"Whatever he wants, whenever he wants," Quint vowed. "If he can get us to Corrie, I don't give a rat's ass what he requires of me."

"And that right there is why Tex is the best," TJ said in a solemn tone. "He's collected markers from a country full of men who are just like you, Quint. But honestly, I know he'd do it just because it's the right thing to do."

TJ's phone vibrated and he quickly tapped it and brought it up to his ear. "Tex…I know, it's been a long time…Corrie Madison, she's blind…Dimitri Prandini, P-r-a-n-d-i-n-i, and Isaac Sampson… Near as we can tell over three hours… Witness says whoever it was that forced her to go to Corrie's house talked about a cabin…Yeah…We'll be waiting." TJ clicked the phone off and turned to his friends.

"Well?"

"He's going to call me back."

"This is ridiculous," Quint barked out, turning to Cruz. "I can't just stand here waiting for some mysterious fucking guy named Tex to find out where Corrie is after a thirty-second phone conversation. Cruz, call your guy at the bureau. Have him search for properties that trace back to Dimitri or Isaac. It's a long shot, but they might be arrogant enough to have taken her to one of their own damn houses."

"Give Tex five minutes, Cruz," TJ ordered. Everyone looked at him in surprise. TJ was the happy-go-lucky one of their group. It was surprising enough that the man had been Delta, he just didn't seem to have the disposition, but one look at his demeanor and countenance at the moment and no one doubted the man was a lethal killer.

"Tex will find her. He's a fucking hacker. I didn't give him much information, but he'll do his magic computer shit and tell us where they are. It'll take Cruz's FBI guy three hours to do what it'll take Tex five minutes to find."

"I can't lose her," Quint said, heartbroken.

"You won't," Daxton assured him with conviction. "These guys are too cocky. They think they're invincible. They've left a trail that this computer geek'll find. Believe it."

No one said anything for several minutes. Quint paced as the other SAPD officers and medical personnel gave the quintet a wide berth. They were obviously putting out some intense vibes because no one bothered them.

Finally, after seven minutes had passed, TJ's phone vibrated with an incoming call. He immediately clicked it on and listened before saying, "All right, give us a second."

TJ motioned for the others to follow him outside. Without asking why, everyone followed the Highway Patrolman until they arrived next to his car, out of the way of others who might overhear their conversation. He clicked the speaker icon on the phone and held it out in the middle of the tight circle of lawmen.

"Okay, go ahead, Tex. We're all here."

"First, I'm sorry as I could be that these assholes got ahold of your woman," Tex said with a hint of a southern drawl. "But the good news is that they aren't very smart. Prandini has several aliases. Prado, Prandino, Prandima...as I said...not very smart. Anyway, looks like the man held a marker for a down-home country boy named Chaz Willis. Chaz had a bit of a gambling problem, but also had some issues on the side with not one, but two ex-wives. He somehow conned his sister-in-law into purchasing a house for him in her name, so his current wife wouldn't be able to find him when he was hooking up with his first ex or his current girlfriend."

"Jesus, is there a point?" Quint asked, stressed beyond control.

"I have a point," Tex said, not seeming to be ruffled at all by Quint's outburst. "It's that Chaz owed Prandini money. Money he didn't have. All of a sudden our friend Chaz hasn't made any trips out to his little hunting cabin at the lake in over a year. Cell phone and credit card records show he's living a perfectly miserable life right there in the heart of San Antonio. There haven't been any 'hunting trips' for the man in all of that time. Oh, and his third divorce is pending."

"Prandini?" Cruz demanded.

"Yup. He's the proud new owner of a small, out-of-the-way cabin on Medina Lake. He's been switching up his credit cards, but there have been gas and food charges awfully close to that area. I have a feeling the man isn't the outdoorsy type."

"Fuck me. Medina Lake," Quint breathed incredulously. "I should've thought of that."

"What's the connection?" Hayden asked.

"Shaun's body was found there," Quint informed the group matter-of-factly.

"Address?" Cruz asked, a pad of paper in his hand, ready to write it down.

"The cabin has a half-mile dirt road leading to it and is surrounded by trees and scrub. As you all know, this has been a warm year for Texas, but there are still lots of places to hide out there. You'll need to go in quiet and sneak up on them."

"Fuck, Tex. Who the hell do you think you're talkin' to here?" Quint groused. "Address?"

"South side. Take PR 2670 off of route 265. Go one-point-two miles north and there's a dirt road on your left. It's down that road. I'll send the coordinates to Rock."

"Let's go, it's at least thirty minutes to get out there," Quint said, turning to head to his truck.

"Quint," Tex called out.

He paused and waited for the man to continue. He was itching to get the hell out of there and get to Corrie, but he owed Tex another couple seconds of his time. If he was right and this is where Corrie was...Quint knew he owed him a lot more than mere time.

"From what I could tell in the five minutes I had to research her, your woman is intelligent. If there's a way out of this, she'll find it."

"Thanks. I'm counting on it." And with that, Quint strode toward Hayden's vehicle. It was a four-wheel drive and they'd decided while they were waiting for Tex to call back, that if needed, they'd take hers since it was more maneuverable in the backcountry of Texas.

He blanked out the others getting into their cars and even his phone vibrating with a text with the coordinates from TJ. All Quint could think about was Corrie. Had too much time passed? Was she all right? What were those pricks doing to her?

Never in his life had he wanted to be a knight in shining armor as badly as he wanted to be one today. It had never been as vital to his well-being as now.

"Hang on, sweetheart. I'm coming for you," he whispered as Hayden pulled away from the curb. "I'm on my way."

CHAPTER 14

CORRIE LAY on the floor where the man had thrown her. She'd awoken in his car. She was disoriented and dizzy, but knew she was in big trouble. She remembered Bethany being at her house, then nothing. Was she okay? Emily? Ethan? Dang it, she hated not knowing, but she'd be damned if she asked her captors.

She'd known the second she woke up that she was in the presence of the man who'd killed Cayley and all the others at the clinic. She recognized his voice, and his nasty smell. That stench was stuck in her nose. She felt a little vindicated, because no matter what the DA thought, even if the woman was thinking about allowing her testimony, she'd *known* she'd be able to pick him out. But vindication at this point wouldn't help her.

The man, Isaac—he'd actually introduced himself to her as if they were at a fancy party—had talked the entire time they'd been in the car. He'd talked in great detail about what he'd done with Shaun, he'd even bragged about his and his boss's plan to bring her out to the middle of nowhere to torture and kill her.

Corrie had wanted to ask about Bethany and Emily, but kept her mouth shut. It seemed to piss him off that he couldn't get her to talk to him, but no matter what vile thing he said, she refused to open her mouth.

They'd driven for what seemed like forever until he'd pulled off on a gravel road. Corrie could tell the difference in the texture of the road under the car's tires. He really was bringing her to the middle of nowhere. She smelled pine trees all around, and dust. It was dry, wherever they were.

Corrie felt a panic attack coming on, but held on to her sanity by the skin of her teeth. She couldn't lose it now. Her parents had trained her to use her senses when she got turned around. This was the same thing. She just had to concentrate.

Isaac had pulled her roughly from the car and hauled her forward, laughing as she tripped over objects in her path. She had no idea where they were or where they were going, but Corrie played up her helplessness as much as she could. She wanted Isaac and his boss to think she was completely unable to help herself in any way.

Isaac had thrown her into a room and slammed the door. Corrie heard the lock being engaged from the other side. She got up and carefully made her way to the door, arms out in front of her to try to keep from running into anything, feeling good about only hitting one chair. She leaned her ear against the wooden door and listened.

"What now, Dimitri?"

"Now we figure out what she knows and what the cops know."

"Then what?"

Corrie heard a smacking sound and Isaac cried out.

"Calm the fuck down. You'll get to stick your dick in her as soon as I know what I want to know."

Corrie didn't like the sound of any of that.

She heard the two men coming back down the hall. Corrie hurried back to the middle of the floor where she'd been thrown and held back a sob. *Where are you, Quint? I need you.*

QUINT HELD on to the safety bar and gritted his

teeth. Hayden drove like a bat out of hell. She didn't even slow down going around corners. The SUV she'd commandeered from her department groaned and made all sorts of god-awful noises as she pushed it to its limit.

All Quint could think about was how scared Corrie probably was. She hadn't even wanted to move into his house because she wasn't sure where all his furniture was. How scared would she have to be now? In the middle of a fucking forest with two psychotic assholes doing who knows what to her? She didn't even have her cane…he'd seen it folded in her purse when he'd gotten her cell phone out.

He ground his teeth together. He'd kill the motherfuckers if they'd touched so much as a hair on her head.

"We're gonna get to her, Quint. Not only us, but I think most of Station 7 is on their way too. You know those firefighters would do anything for you." Hayden said calmly from next to him. He looked over at her. She seemed to be calm, cool, and collected, even as she drove like she was competing in the Indianapolis 500.

"Yeah," was all Quint could squeeze out between his clenched teeth. He was happy the EMTs were on their way too, Corrie might need them, but he hated the thought of her even having a papercut. This was torture. They'd get to her all right. It was what they'd find when they got there that worried him.

* * *

CORRIE TRIED to ignore the adrenaline coursing through her body and pretended as if she was a helpless female. "I don't know what you're talking about. I didn't see anything! I didn't hear anything but gunshots. I don't know why the cops think I can tell one person from another. I'm bliiiiind." She whined the word, trying to sound even more pathetic. "I didn't see *anyone*."

"Jesus fucking Christ," Dimitri bitched, pacing back and forth in front of the chair they'd plunked her in. "She doesn't know shit. We've spent all this time and money for nothing."

Corrie shook her head, trying to clear the ringing from her ears. Her face hurt from where Isaac had clocked her earlier at the house, and again from where both Dimitri and Isaac had taken turns slapping and hitting her to try to figure out what she knew. The idiots hadn't even bothered to tie her to the chair, thinking she was a pitiful, helpless, blind female—thank God.

"Can I have her now then?"

Corrie heard Dimitri's fist hitting Isaac's face

again. "You are such a fucking horn-dog. We have damage control to do first, asshole. Leave her alone. You'll get your fuck later, then you can get rid of her. And this time, you'll do it right. Not like that fucker Shaun."

Isaac laughed and Corrie flinched and cried out involuntarily as a foot made contact with her knee. Darn, that hurt. She leaned over and wailed excessively, trying to show both men she was out of it, emotionally and physically.

"Come on, we have shit to do," Dimitri said, walking to the door to her room.

Corrie held her breath. *Please don't leave me alone with Isaac. Please don't leave me alone with Isaac.*

"I'll be back, bitch. Hope you're ready for me to shove my big cock up your asshole. I like to start there because it hurts the most. Then I'll move on to your cunt and your face. I love watching as I shove my dick down a chick's throat. Did you know the last woman I killed, I did it by strangling her with my dick? She looked up at me while my cock was down her throat, she couldn't breathe and she died with my jizz coating her stomach. I can't fucking wait."

Isaac slammed the door behind him and Corrie heard him lock it.

Lord. Her hands trembled imagining every

horrible thing he wanted to do to her. She held her hand over her mouth, trying not to throw up. She couldn't lose it now. She took a couple of deep breaths. Thank God he'd left her alone and thank God they hadn't tied her up. She had to get out of here. She couldn't wait for Quint to find her; she didn't think he was going to make it in time. Isaac was way too determined to rape and kill her. It was up to her to save herself.

She heard Isaac and Dimitri arguing in the next room, and it gave her even more incentive to try to escape while they were preoccupied.

Corrie got up, wincing as her knee almost gave out on her. Darn it. One of the men had kicked her harder than she'd thought. The tears that came to her eyes were real this time, not faked. Corrie refused to let them fall and hobbled around the room, hands out in front of her, trying not to run into anything and bring attention to herself.

Her shin hit a table, then a chair, then a bed, but she kept going. The small pains didn't matter, it was better than being dead or brutally violated.

She felt along the wall, breathing a sigh of relief when she found what she was looking for. A window. It was about three feet by three feet, plenty big enough for her to squeeze through. It was around five feet off the floor, which would make it tricky to get up and out of, but she tried to open it.

It didn't budge.

Panic set in and Corrie wasted a bit of time huffing and puffing and straining helplessly to push the window open. Finally she stopped to think and felt for a lock. There! She turned the knob at the top of the window and tried again, pushing slowly.

It moved. Oh my God, it freaking moved.

Corrie continued to push open the window slowly in case it made any noise. It didn't. Thank goodness for owners who took care of their properties. Corrie could hear Isaac and Dimitri still arguing in the other room, so she continued making her escape. Finally the window wouldn't go up any more. Corrie felt with her hands. It wasn't open all the way, but it'd have to do. Remembering the chair, she bent over and shuffled back to where she thought it was.

Bingo. Her fingers made contact with the back and she almost knocked it over. She panted through her terror, knowing if Isaac heard anything suspicious, he'd be back in the room in a heartbeat and she'd lose her chance to get out of there. She carefully picked up the chair, thankful it was a flimsy wooden piece of crap.

Carrying it carefully back to the window, Corrie

put it down and climbed up. Hopefully she'd have enough of a head start before Isaac came back to rape her.

Pausing, Corrie took a few precious seconds to draw seventeen dots on the wall next to the window before she escaped her prison. She'd found and pocketed a pen when she was searching the room earlier, and while she knew she was taking a chance —a big chance that she'd take too long—she had to do it.

Finished, she put the pen inside the window sill, and stuck her head out of the little window and waited. She tilted her head, listening. She could hear the wind blowing, smell pine and decaying leaves, but nothing else. It was now or never.

Corrie pulled herself through the window head first. She lay on her stomach on the sill and put her hands out. She couldn't touch the ground. Darn. She'd hoped that maybe she'd get lucky and there'd be some sort of hill or the ground would be built up next to the house. She had no idea how far it was to the grass below, but since she hadn't gone up any stairs when Isaac was dragging her into the house, she hoped she didn't have too far to fall.

She put her hands on the sill again and wiggled until she was precariously balanced on her hipbones. Corrie put her hands out again and wiggled one more time. Gravity did the rest of the work for her. She fell out of the window and landed hard on her hands. Her elbows gave out and she hit her head as her body crashed to the ground.

Corrie didn't wait to take stock. She picked herself up and started walking quickly toward the smell of the trees. She kept her hands in front of her, used exaggerated steps to walk, and stayed hunched over, trying not to trip over anything in her way. She knew she probably looked ridiculous, but without her cane, it was really hard to walk in unfamiliar places. She knew she was moving way too slowly, but it wasn't like she could just run off. She had to be smart and careful. She only had one chance. If they caught her, she was as good as dead.

No matter what, she had to keep going. No matter how many times she fell, no matter how many times she ran into things…the key to staying alive was putting one foot in front of the other. All she had to do was picture what Isaac wanted to do to her, and it gave her the motivation she needed to keep going.

She was scared to death, this was not fun, and she'd once had nightmares about this exact situation…being lost in the woods.

But Corrie kept going. Step by painfully slow step. Once she got away from the house, she'd figure out what to do next. Corrie knew she just had to stay away from Isaac. Quint would find her eventually. She just had to find the perfect hiding spot. She knew what she was looking for, but it was a crap-shoot as to whether she could actually find it.

She stumbled on, hoping just once that luck was on her side.

"No matter what, you can't lose your shit," Hayden warned as they closed in on the cabin. They'd turned off onto a gravel road. Hayden slowed down only enough so they wouldn't lose a wheel on the deep ruts in the road.

"I'm not going to lose my shit."

"I've read the file on this Isaac guy. We both know what we might find."

Quint ground his teeth together and didn't respond.

"If she's been raped, you have to keep it together," Hayden said stubbornly. "She might not want to be touched. Sometimes even the slightest touch can drive a woman deep into her mind. Just let me see where her head's at before you grab her. If needed, Penelope can help her rather than one of the other male firefighters."

"Shut up."

"Quint, I'm not saying this to hurt you, but you might have to treat her with care."

Quint turned to Hayden. His voice was low and even and only cracked once. "I know exactly what I might find. I might find her scared out of her mind and so far into herself I can't get in. I could find her beaten unconscious, or crucified to a fucking wall. I'm hoping she's still alive. I can deal with anything but that. There's no telling what those assholes could've done to her by now. She's fragile and I'm hanging on by a thread here. So you telling me that asshole might have stuck his cock inside what's mine is *not* helping. I know you mean well, and I appreciate it. I do. But I'd appreciate it more if you could get us the fuck there so I can find my woman and take care of her. Okay?"

"Okay. But Quint?"

He grunted in response.

"I think you're underestimating her. I don't know Corrie, but from what you've told me, I don't think she's all that fragile. She's lived her entire life blind. This isn't new for her. She's been in scary situations before."

"Not like this."

"You're absolutely right, not like this. But you're talking about her as if she sits at home scared to leave the house every day. She has a career. From what you tell me, one she fought like hell to have. She had the presence of mind to hide from Sampson when he shot up her clinic. Remember what Penelope went through over in Turkey. Women are a lot tougher than we seem. Don't sell Corrie short."

Quint could feel his throat closing up. He didn't answer, merely nodded. He hoped Hayden was right. He hoped like hell she was right.

The cab of the SUV was silent the rest of the way to the cabin.

* * *

CORRIE'S HANDS HURT. She knew they were scraped up, and she'd hit her head, hard, on a low branch, but she kept going. Her knee was still throbbing from where she'd been kicked, but she kept hobbling on. She was probably covered in dirt and blood. From the injuries Isaac and Dimitri had given her before she'd gotten out of the cabin, to now, she knew she had to look like an escaped inmate from Laurel Ridge, the psychiatric hospital in San Antonio.

She stopped every now and then and cocked her head to listen, to see if Isaac or Dimitri had realized she was gone yet. So far it was quiet behind her. She had no idea how far she'd gotten, only that it wasn't far enough. It'd probably never be far enough. She had to find what she was looking for soon, otherwise it'd be too late.

She started forward again and before she'd gone a dozen steps, she stopped abruptly. She heard yelling from back the way she'd come. Crap. They'd figured out she was gone.

Corrie walked faster, her heart beating hard. She had to hide. She needed to find the perfect place to hide...*now*.

Corrie bounced off what felt like the fiftieth tree since she'd left the cabin and hit the ground hard. She panted for a moment. Why in the world did she think she'd be able to pull this off? Fuck, she wasn't comfortable negotiating herself in a strange room, nevertheless in the middle of a fucking forest.

She sobbed once. Great. Just great. Now she was swearing *and* crying. She got to her feet and put her hands out in front of her again. She just had to keep going. One step at a time. She wasn't going to make it easy for those assholes. If they wanted her, they'd have to fight for her.

She stepped forward another dozen steps and ran into something. Darn it. Another freaking tree.

Wait... She felt this one.

Oh my God, it seemed perfect.

There was a limb close enough to the ground that

she could grab it. That had been her plan from the second she'd decided to crawl out the window, and this was the first tree that it seemed might work. She grabbed the first branch, which was around shoulder height, and put her knee on the trunk to help her climb. She pulled herself up, trying not to grunt with the effort it took. Her arms shook, but she didn't give up. Finally she managed to haul herself up on top of that first limb. Corrie put one hand above her head, thanking God there was another branch there, and slowly pulled herself up. She only got to a crouch before she hit another limb. Bingo.

She felt around her and stepped up to the next branch. She continued climbing. Slowly but surely. She could feel the tree she was in swaying gently in the breeze, but she didn't stop. She had no idea how high she'd climbed, but she knew she had to keep going. She had to get high enough that Isaac and Dimitri couldn't see her. She prayed there were leaves on this tree to hide her; she thought there were because she could hear the rustling in the air that blew around her. Even if they saw her, they'd have to climb up to get her. Dying from falling out of this tree would be better than whatever Isaac had in store for her.

Finally, when the limbs seemed too skinny and frail to be able to hold her weight if she stepped on them, she halted her frantic upward climb. She hugged the trunk of the tree tightly and tried to calm her breathing. It wouldn't be much of a hiding place if she gave herself away by panting too loud.

Corrie knew she was high. The sound of leaves rustling made her feel hopeful that she was sufficiently covered. The trunk she was gripping wasn't that wide this high up, her arms fit all the way around it with room to spare. Even though it made no difference, she squeezed her eyes shut, praying she couldn't be seen from the ground.

She wasn't sure how long she'd been clinging to the tree like a frightened monkey, but all of a sudden the silence around her was broken by Isaac and Dimitri's voices as they made their way toward her. They were moving much quicker than she had.

"Come out, come out, wherever you are," Isaac taunted in a singsong voice that would surely give children nightmares rather than soothe them. "You might as well come out now. We know you came this way because we saw your fucking footprints leading right into the woods. If you give yourself up now, I promise to go easy on you."

Corrie stayed silent.

"Come on, sweet cheeks. You're not going to get away from us. You're fucking blind. You're gonna lose. If you yell out now, I'll kill you quickly."

Dimitri's voice cut through Isaac's fake pleasant tone. "Get out here, bitch! You're gonna fucking pay for this. No one makes a fool out of Dimitri Prandini."

Corrie shivered at the hate and insanity in his voice. She trembled as she adjusted her grip. She held her breath as the men seemed to stop right below the tree she was hiding in. She felt exactly like she had that day so many weeks ago when she knew if she made one wrong move, or one wrong sound, she'd die.

Exactly like that.

"We don't have time for this shit, Dimitri."

"We aren't leaving her. She could ruin everything."

"They're not going to take a blind bitch's word that I was the one who shot those fucking people."

"I don't give a fuck about you taking the rap for that! I care about her getting away and being charged with attempted murder, kidnapping, and you being a pussy in interrogation and fingering me for Shaun's death as well."

"I wouldn't turn against you, Dimitri."

"The fuck you wouldn't."

"Look, you know I want that bitch more than anyone. Not only did she manage to hide from me, but I'll be dammed if I go to jail because of some handicapped blonde whore. I agree that we need to find her, but we can't stay out here all night. She can't have gone far. She's blind, for Christ's sake. Where else would she go out here? Let's keep looking for a bit longer. She's bound to trip over something and hurt herself badly enough so she can't get up. We'll bring her back to the house, I'll fuck her, you'll torture her, then we'll kill her. I'll be sure to dispose of her body so that no one will ever find any trace of her."

"You fucked this up, Isaac! Leaving her in a room with a damn window. I think she's more resourceful than you gave her credit for! Her ass needs to die. Maybe she could've identified you, maybe she couldn't, but she most certainly can *now*. She's heard us talk; she knows what we were planning. We can't let her escape now. No fucking way."

"Dammit. Fucking bitch. It's getting dark. We've got those high-powered flashlights in the car…let's go back and get them. There's no way she'll be able to spend the night out here alone. She'll most likely try to make her way toward the road. If she gets there and is able to flag down a car, we're screwed."

Corrie heard the two men walking back toward the way they came, but she didn't dare move. She let out her breath slowly as the men's voices got softer as they headed back to get their lights so they could continue to search for her. She had no idea what she'd do if they found her, or how they would get her out of the tree. Corrie wasn't planning on coming down anytime soon, they'd have to climb up and get her, or chop the tree down. She wasn't moving. No way, no how.

As the adrenaline in her body receded, she began to shake. Soon, she couldn't tell what was the wind, and what was her trembling muscles. It didn't matter. She wasn't budging. She'd stay right where she was until Quint found her, even if she had to spend the night out there. She had no doubt Quint would come for her. No doubt at all.

QUINT, Dax, Hayden, TJ, Cruz, and six other officers from both the SAPD and the FBI crept through the trees toward the cabin. They'd left their vehicles about half a mile down the gravel road so as not to alert Isaac and Dimitri they were coming. There were two trucks from Station 7 firestation on stand-by as well as an ambulance.

There was a black SUV parked in front of the cabin, so hopefully that meant the men were still there. The group of law enforcement officers split up and surrounded the house. Isaac and Dimitri weren't going to get away. No fucking way.

Quint wanted to rush the cabin and get to Corrie, but knew they had to move slowly and carefully. One wrong move could force either of the men to kill her outright before they could get to her. He wouldn't put it past them.

"Window open on the west side," Quint heard Cruz say in a deep voice through his earpiece.

"Front door standing open," Hayden replied in a steady voice from the other side of the cabin.

Quint and TJ turned together when they heard voices coming from behind them. They rushed to the other side of the SUV to conceal themselves and watched incredulously as Isaac and Dimitri came walking out of the woods—as if they'd been on a nice leisurely stroll through the trees and hadn't just kidnapped a woman and almost killed two others.

"Hurry up and get them. We need to take care of this once and for all. We're one step ahead of the pig cops right now, and need to keep them off our asses as much as possible. After she's disposed of, we'll hit up some of our other clients and get the fuck out of here. We can lay low and re-group. A blind woman isn't going to be the end of my business. No fucking way!" Dimitri bitched as he sauntered next to Isaac.

The men were almost to the SUV when TJ

popped up from around the front of their car, his pistol pointed at Dimitri. "Sorry, guys, the pig cops are all *over* your asses."

Quint would've rolled his eyes at the corny joke, but he couldn't muster the wherewithal to do it. Where were these assholes coming from and where was Corrie?

Isaac and Dimitri turned to run back into the woods, and came face-to-face with four more officers with guns. They were completely surrounded.

Isaac, obviously the more impulsive of the two, decided to make a grand gesture and pulled a pistol out of the holster at his side.

Several shots rang out through the clearing despite Quint's demand to hold fire. Within seconds, neither Isaac nor Dimitri would ever collect another dime from anyone again.

Quint didn't give a fuck whose bullets actually ended the slimeballs' lives, except for the fact that they might have been the only two people on the earth who knew where Corrie was. They'd been talking about disposing her body, and that alone almost destroyed him. He tried to stay positive and hope that they hadn't gotten around to killing her yet.

Hayden put her pistol back into her holster. She shrugged her shoulders at Quint before they turned to run toward the house to look for Corrie. "Two less cockroaches to worry about." She really was hard-core, right down to her bones.

Quint holstered his own smoking service pistol as he sprinted toward the open door to the cabin.

He walked briskly through the small cabin. Every room was empty. Standing in one of the small bedrooms, he turned to TJ, who'd followed him inside.

"Quint…" TJ shook his head sadly.

Quint held up his palm to his friend. "No. Fucking no. I won't believe she's dead until I see it with my own eyes."

"Buddy, they were coming back from the woods."

Suddenly Dax was there. He put his hand on TJ's shoulder. "No. Quint's right. Until we see her, she's not dead. Remember Mack? I watched her die, but she's still with me today. We continue on until there's absolutely no hope, then we continue on some more."

TJ nodded solemnly. "Fuck. Yeah, you're right. Let's re-search. There has to be something here."

The men split up. Dax and TJ went back to the main part of the house and Quint looked around the rooms in the back. He searched the first room with no luck, but as he headed toward the second room, he took another glance at the door.

Yes! There was a brand-new knob on the door, but it was installed backwards. The lock was on the outside, not the inside of the room. He went in and looked around. How the fuck had he missed it the first time?

He'd been looking for Corrie, not clues, that's how.

This was the room with the open window. There was a chair sitting under it. Quint scanned the room. It seemed to be nothing out of the ordinary. A twin bed, a dresser, a small closet, and that chair. He looked more carefully.

A pen. There was a pen in the windowsill.

Adrenaline coursed through Quint's body. "Dax!" he yelled, even as he walked to the window to take a closer look. Just as Dax was striding into the room, Quint saw it.

Small dots on the wall.

She'd left him a fucking message.

"What is it?" Dax asked, coming up beside Quint.

"Braille."

"What's it say?"

Quint ran his fingers over the dots. They weren't raised like Braille was, but he couldn't stop himself from touching them. His Corrie had been there and left them for him. He tried to concentrate on the message she'd left for him.

"Well?" Dax asked impatiently.

"Give me a second. I'm new at this. O, V, T...no, wait...U. O, U, T. Out."

"Out? Okay, with the chair sitting right there it's obvious she went out the window. Is that it?"

"No, there's more." Quint tilted his head to look at the last two letters. She'd used Grade 1 Braille to spell out the letters. She probably knew he was still trying to get the hang of Grade 2 and didn't want to risk him not understanding what she wanted to tell him.

U and...P. Up.

"Out and Up. She went out and we need to look up."

"Did your blind girlfriend really jump out a window in the middle of a forest after being kidnapped and head off to try to find a fucking tree to climb?"

Quint smiled at Dax's words. Hayden had been right. Women *were* tough as shit. It was the first time he'd allowed himself to relax since he'd heard Corrie was missing. "Yeah. I think she did."

"Damn, I like her, Quint. Anyone who can rescue herself is totally worthy of you."

"Yeah, I like her too. Now, can we go and find my woman and get the fuck out of here?" Quint was already on the move as he said the words. Dax was right behind him. They collected TJ, Cruz, and Hayden on their way out.

The five officers gathered next to the cabin under the open window. Quint looked around. He closed his eyes, put his arms out and started walking.

He didn't get ten feet before he opened his eyes. He couldn't do it. He had no idea how Corrie had found the strength and courage to walk, literally blind into the forest. He couldn't make it past ten steps.

Hayden had been completely right in chastising him for underestimating Corrie. She wasn't fragile, not in the way he'd been thinking. He had no doubt everything that had happened today would traumatize her, but he'd be damned if he ever disparaged her again by thinking she was weak.

He continued walking forward, alternating between looking down and looking up. He'd be the first person to tell her how proud he was of her...as soon as he found her.

CHAPTER 15

CORRIE SHIVERED. She didn't think it was cold outside, but she couldn't really tell. She couldn't feel her feet; the thin branch she was standing on had cut off her circulation. Climbing a tree in flip-flops wasn't the smartest thing she'd ever done, but it wasn't as if she'd had a choice.

Her head and knee hurt where Isaac and Dimitri had hit her. She felt dizzy, but wasn't sure if it was because of the swaying of the tree she was in, or something else. She shivered and hugged the tree tighter. The last thing she needed was to fall out before Quint found her. She just wished he'd hurry up.

She dozed off for a bit, but she woke up with a start and convulsively grabbed at the tree. She sighed in relief when she didn't fall. She leaned her forehead against the scratchy bark and tried not to cry.

"Coooooorrie!"

Corrie lifted her head and tilted it in the hopes of hearing better.

"Coooooorrie. Where are you?"

Her heart started beating like a jackrabbit again. Was Isaac back already? Darn it, she hoped maybe they'd give up the idea of looking for her when they got back to their car. Maybe the batteries in the flashlights would be dead or something. She kept her mouth shut and tried to slow her breathing.

"Corrie? Are you out here?"

The voice was female. Corrie didn't understand what was going on. Had Dimitri and Isaac come back with reinforcements? Did they kidnap another woman? She was so confused.

She could hear more voices now. They were muted so she couldn't catch their words.

"Corrie, sweetheart…can you hear me? It's Quint. You're safe."

Quint? Quint was finally here! His voice echoed around the trees and blew into the wind.

Corrie looked toward the ground. It was silly; it wasn't as if she could see anything. She waited. The voices got closer and closer.

What if it was a trap? What if Dimitri had a gun

to Quint's head or something? He could be using Quint to flush her out.

For the first time in a really long time, Corrie wished she could see. She used to pray to God to give her sight when she was little, but now she really *really* wished she could see what was going on because if she got Quint killed, she would hate herself for all eternity.

She had to take a chance. Would all those people be with him if Isaac had him? She hoped not. "Quint?" Her voice came out as a croak. She tried again, stronger this time. "Quint? I'm here."

"Corrie? Thank fucking God!"

Corrie almost laughed at the relief in his voice.

"Again, talk to me again so I can find you."

Corrie swallowed down the tears clogging her throat. "Here. I'm up in a tree."

"Keep talking, sweetheart. We'll find you."

We? She didn't care who was with him. She couldn't wait for him to hold her. "I'm up here. I climbed as high as I could so they couldn't see me. I have no idea how high I am though. Can you see me yet?" The last part came out way too pathetic-sounding for her peace of mind.

Quint stopped beneath the tall tree and stared up. He could barely see Corrie. Good God. He had no idea how she'd even gotten up that high. How in the hell was he going to get her down? "I see you, sweetheart. You just keep hanging on, okay?"

"Quint? Are you okay? They're not with you?"

He immediately understood. Figured she'd be worried about him and not herself. "No, Corrie. They're not here. I'm here with Cruz and some of my other friends. You're safe."

"Did you get them? Their names are Isaac and Dimitri, they killed Shaun. They were going to kill me too, but I got away. Did you get my message?"

Quint's heart hurt. Corrie sounded so sad and lost. He wanted nothing more than to grab hold of her and never let go. "We got them, sweetheart. They won't hurt you or anyone else again. They were shot and killed back at the cabin. And yes, I got your message." He tried to interject some humor into their conversation, even though he wasn't really feeling it. "And so you know, your U looks like a V."

"It does not," she protested weakly. "You just need more practice."

Quint snorted and started undoing his shirt. He'd need to take off his vest and belt in order to be able to get through the thick network of branches to get to her.

"I got this."

He turned to see Hayden had already taken off her gear and was reading to shimmy up the tree. He put a hand on her arm. "No, she's my responsibility, I'll go up."

"There's no way you'll fit, Quint, think about it. I grew up climbing trees like this. Besides, you weigh more than me or Corrie. You'll possibly break the branches and she'll be stuck up there. Trust me. I'll bring her to you safely."

Quint hated it with every fiber of his being, but Hayden was right, dammit. "Okay, but," he didn't take his eyes off of Hayden's, "be careful. She means the world to me."

Hayden simply nodded and demanded, "Give me a boost."

Quint put his hands together and held them down for her to step into. She did and he hoisted her easily up to the first branch. Looking at it, Quint had no idea how Corrie had managed to haul herself up there with no help. "Help's coming, Corrie. Hang on."

"You're coming up to get me?"

Quint could hear the hope in her voice and hated to disappoint her. "No, not me. I'm too big. But Hayden's coming. Remember me telling you about her? She's a sheriff's deputy and can outshoot and outrun most of the guys in my department. And whatever you do, don't challenge her to one-on-one combat. She's the only woman I know who can manage to flip me." Quint kept his words calm and soothing. He could tell Corrie was on the verge of freaking out. "Corrie?"

"Yeah, okay. I'm scared. I've been waiting for you, why'd you take so long?" Corrie hated the wobble in her voice, but she'd been brave for as long as she could be, and now that Quint was there, she allowed herself to fall apart...just a little. She'd added the last to try to keep herself from freaking out more.

"I know you are, but I'm so fucking proud of you. You have no idea." Quint kept his eye on Hayden as she shimmied up the tree as if she'd been born in one. "I set off to find you and closed my eyes for about two-point-three seconds before I had to open them again. I couldn't do it. But you did, sweetheart. You did it. You outsmarted those assholes and saved yourself. You didn't need me to do it."

"I—" Her voice cut off. Quint could see that Hayden had made her way to Corrie and was talking to her.

* * *

CORRIE JERKED AWAY from the touch on her calf, then relaxed when she heard the female voice.

"Easy, Corrie. It's me, Hayden Yates. I'm going to help you down. All right?"

Corrie nodded. "Okay, thank you. I had no idea how in the heck I was gonna get out of here. How high am I?"

"You did a good job, and you don't want to know how far you climbed, but it was high enough that we almost couldn't see you from the ground. Even if those assholes stood right under you, they probably wouldn't have seen you."

"I think they *did* stand right under me."

"Ha, well fuck them then. Come on. I'm going to take hold of your sweats and guide your foot to a branch. Your shoes aren't going to make this easy, but we'll take this slow and steady. Take your time, there's absolutely no rush. No bad guys are waiting, only Quint, and he can just cool his jets down there…right?"

Corrie smiled, realizing Hayden was trying to relax her. She nodded again.

"Okay, this first step is easy. The branch is about six inches below your right foot. Just shift your hold on the trunk and ease your foot down. That's it."

Corrie followed Hayden's gentle pressure on her sweats and moved her foot carefully. The branch was exactly where she said it'd be.

"Good, now move your left foot the same way. It'll fit right next to your other one on the same branch."

Corrie did as directed and took a deep breath. Okay, she could do this.

They continued their slow and steady pace down the tree until they got to a tricky part. Corrie remembered this particular gap in the branches as she'd climbed up.

"Okay, this is the last of the hard parts, Corrie. It's about a four-foot gap between where you're standing now and where the next branch is below you. You're going to need to crouch down, leaving one foot on the branch and reaching down with your other one. It'll be a stretch, but your legs are long enough to reach. Promise. I'll help guide you so your foot will go right where it's supposed to."

Corrie nodded. She'd come this far. She circled the trunk of the tree with her arms and bent her legs. She moved her left foot until it dangled down. She felt Hayden's grip on her ankle.

"Just a bit more, that's it. Almost there…"

Just as Corrie thought she felt the branch under her foot, her right foot slipped off the branch it was on.

She screeched and knocked her forehead on a branch at her head level as she felt herself falling. Her shin whacked against the limb she'd been standing on and she gripped the broad trunk of the tree for dear life. "Shit!"

"Corrie!" Quint's voice was frantic.

Hayden's voice came below her. It was calm and even, as if she hadn't just watched her almost fall out of the stupid tree. Corrie could feel the strong and secure grip the other woman had on her ankle. Hayden held her steady as she knelt on the limb like an idiot.

"No problem, Corrie. Just a small slip. You're okay."

"That's the second time I've sworn today, darn it. That's not cool."

Hayden chuckled. "You're crackin' me up. I think you have a right to say a swear word or two."

Corrie shook her head. "No, I promised myself when Ethan, my friend's kid, was born that I'd stop. I was a complete potty mouth before. I had to go cold turkey or his first word was bound to be a swear-word he learned from his Aunt Corrie."

"Come on, you're almost there. Trust me. Give me some of your weight and I'll guide your foot to the next branch."

Corrie took a deep breath and did as Hayden asked. She wanted out of this darn tree and the only way to do that was to get past this section. She eased off her shin and felt Hayden guide her foot, exactly as she'd promised. Corrie felt the sturdy limb under her foot and breathed a sigh of relief.

"Okay, I've got you, slide your other leg off and grab hold of the branch it was just resting on with your hands."

Corrie felt one of Hayden's hands on her lower back and the other on her calf. She shifted and Hayden moved the hand that was on her right calf to her hip. "There you go. Good. Piece of cake. We're only about eight feet from the ground, and Quint is waiting for you. Only about two more steps and he'll have his hands on you. Ready?"

Corrie nodded eagerly, more than ready.

They moved quickly past the next couple of branches and just as Hayden had said, Corrie felt large hands grasp her around her waist. She hadn't felt anything as wonderful as Quint's arms coming around her.

"Thank God," Corrie heard Quint mutter as he lifted her out of the tree and into his arms. She heard a thud as Hayden jumped out of the tree herself. She knew she should thank the deputy, but being in Quint's arms, smelling his unique smell, was more than she could take after everything that had happened.

Corrie burst into tears and buried her face in Quint's neck. She felt his hand cradle the back of her head as he held her against him.

Quint dipped his head and breathed into Corrie's

hair as he hugged her. "You're okay, sweetheart. I've got you. You're good." He continued to whisper nonsense as he followed his friends back through the woods to their vehicles. Corrie vaguely realized she probably should've at least said hello to the other men who were with Quint, but she couldn't seem to stop crying long enough to manage it. She heard them talking as they walked, but couldn't concentrate on their words.

Their little group quickly reached the clearing and Quint didn't even pause to look at the dead bodies lying near the black SUV. Someone had collected the police and fire vehicles from down the road and they were lined up and waiting.

Quint kept Corrie's head against his neck and headed straight for Hayden's SUV. He leaned down and managed to open the door without letting go of Corrie. He sat on the seat sideways and propped his feet on the running board. His heart hurt as Corrie cried in his arms. After a few minutes, she hiccuped and he could tell she was trying to bring herself under control.

He looked down at her and grimaced in sympathy. She had a scrape on her forehead, probably from when she'd almost fallen out of the tree on her way down. There were bruises forming on her jaw and cheekbone. Her hair was a mess and she had dirt smeared from her nose to her ears.

She'd never looked more beautiful to him.

"I love you, Corrie Madison." Quint couldn't have kept the words back if his life depended on it. "I've never been so scared in all my life than when I realized you were gone. I don't want to go through this crazy life without you. I don't care how long it takes, I'm going to show you day in and day out how much you mean to me in the hopes that you'll eventually love me back. I…"

He paused. Corrie had lifted her hand to his neck and was tapping against him. Two diagonal taps, then three vertical taps, then five taps in a backward C shape. She did it again. Then again.

He smiled, and it was his turn to bury his nose in her neck. "You love me?" he mumbled against her.

"Yeah." Corrie sniffed. She knew she probably looked like death warmed over, but Quint didn't seem to care. "When I was stumbling blindly through the woods looking for a tree to climb, all I could think of was how much I loved you and how sad I was that I hadn't told you. But you know what else?"

She felt Quint raise his head. "What?"

"I knew you'd come for me. No matter what. I was going to hang on to the top of that darn tree forever if it took that long, because I knew you'd figure it out and find me."

"Lord, Corrie."

She thought about something suddenly. "Oh no! Bethany…is she okay? What about Emily and Ethan? I don't remember what happened."

Quint ran his hand over her hair again, soothing her. "They're fine. I'll tell you everything later, but they're fine."

"Promise?"

"Yeah. Promise."

Corrie snuggled into Quint, grumbling about the hard bulletproof vest for the first time. She hadn't noticed it before, but now she wanted him. Just him.

"Corrie? My friends Sledge and Crash are here. They're firefighters and EMTs. They just want to take a quick look to make sure you're all right."

Corrie didn't even move from her position curled around Quint. "I'm fine."

"I know you are, but I'd still feel better if you'd let them check you over."

"We're not so bad, promise," a deep voice said from beside her.

A second voice chimed in as well, "Yeah, although I'm the good-looking one."

Corrie turned her head and tried to get herself back together. "Sledge and Crash?" she questioned.

"Long story. Does anything hurt?"

Ten minutes later, assured that Corrie really was okay, other than being scared and some minor scrapes and bruises that would fade and eventually heal, Quint stood up with Corrie in his arms. He nodded at Sledge and Crash, and gave a thankful chin lift to Penelope, Chief and Moose, other firefighters from Station 7 who were standing next to the trucks, in case they were needed.

"You guys ready to go?" Hayden asked as she opened the driver's side door.

"Yeah."

"Great, but you can't hold her like that, Quint. You know the law. Safety first."

Corrie laughed at the disgruntled noise that came from Quint's throat. "We have to sit in the back, don't we?"

Quint's answer was to stand up without letting go of Corrie. He shut the front door with his hip and opened the back door. He sat down, still holding on to her, and hauled Corrie over his lap and placed her in the seat next to him. He pulled the seat belt over her waist and then buckled his own. Ignoring the stretch of the material over his shoulder, he pulled Corrie into the crook of his arm and relaxed as she melted against him.

"Take us home, Hayden."

CHAPTER 16

"ARE you sure you're all right?" Corrie asked Bethany for what seemed like the hundredth time.

Quint had Hayden take them straight to the hospital. Corrie had tried to insist she didn't need to see a doctor, especially since his friends had looked her over and said they thought she was fine, but Quint didn't care. He trusted Sledge and Crash, but they weren't doctors. He told Corrie she could have internal injuries that she simply didn't realize because of the adrenaline coursing through her body. It wasn't until he'd told her what had happened to Emily, Bethany, and Ethan that'd she'd agreed—hell, she insisted.

Quint had refused to let her see her friends until a doctor had checked her out. She sat still...barely...

and answered the doctor's questions with ill-concealed impatience.

"Ms. Madison, besides some scrapes and bruises, I'd say you are one very lucky woman."

"Okay, great." Corrie had turned to where Quint was standing. "I told you so…and so did Crash and Sledge. Will you take me to see Bethany *now*?"

Quint had resisted chuckling, knowing it would irritate Corrie and probably put him in the dog house. "Yeah, sweetheart. Thanks, Dr. Davis. I appreciate you taking a look. I don't know what I'd do without her."

Corrie had squeezed Quint's arm, acknowledging his sweet words, but then ruined it by huffing, "If I could find her by myself, I'd do it, but since I'd probably keep running into people and walls, I need you to show me where my friends are."

The doctor had nodded at Quint and smirked. Quint just ignored the older man and took Corrie's hand in his and set out to find her friends.

The second Corrie had walked into the hospital room where Bethany was recuperating, Emily, who was also visiting, burst into tears. Emily had rushed into Corrie's arms and they spent more than a few minutes enjoying the feel of each other alive and well.

Corrie put her hands on Emily's face and ran her fingers over it. "Does it hurt?"

Emily laughed a watery laugh. "About as much as yours does, I'd imagine."

Corrie grimaced in commiseration.

"Hey, you two, I'm the one in the hospital bed here."

Corrie rushed over and asked if she was okay.

"I'm good. Are you sure you don't hate me, Cor? I didn't want to do it…but he threatened Ethan."

"Lord, Bethany. Of *course* I don't hate you. God, I would've done the same thing. You did the right thing, and besides, it all turned out fine in the end. I'm just sorry you both got sucked into the entire thing. If it wasn't for me—"

Both Emily and Quint spoke at once, interrupting her.

"That's not—"

"Don't." Quint's word was louder. He spoke over whatever Emily was going to say. "This is not your fault. If you want to blame someone, blame Isaac. Or Dimitri, or even Shaun, but there's no way I'll let you blame yourself."

"But—"

Quint shut Corrie up the only way he knew how. He swooped down and covered her mouth with his own. He dimly heard both Emily and Bethany catcalling, but he didn't stop. He thrust his tongue into her mouth, more relieved than he was willing to admit out loud when she returned his kiss. He'd been afraid she'd be too scared with everything that had happened to return his passion. He should've known better.

He finally raised his head and nuzzled against the side of Corrie's neck as he tried to rein in the urgent need to get her alone and show her just how much she meant to him, and to relieve some of the stress he'd been feeling since finding out she'd been kidnapped.

"In case you're wondering, Ethan is fine."

Corrie spun at Emily's teasing words, almost clipping Quint's chin in the process. "Ethan! Where is he? He's really okay? I'm a horrible aunt for not even *asking* about him!"

Quint stood behind Corrie and put his hands around her waist. He pulled her into him, loving the way she trusted him to take her weight.

"Calm down, Cor. He's fine. He was checked out and didn't even have a scratch on him. Thank God Quint realized something was wrong and showed up when he did. He was a little cold, but otherwise fine." Bethany's words were strong and sure.

Emily sat down in the chair next to Bethany and stroked her forearm above the bandages covering her hand. Quint knew Bethany had a long road to recovery ahead of her…some of the nerves in her hand had been severed and there were lots of surgeries in her future.

"My mom came and took him home with her for the night," Emily explained.

"Your mom? But she doesn't approve—"

"I know. But apparently a psycho beating me up and almost killing my partner and son made her think twice about everything."

"It's about darn time."

Emily simply laughed. "So, now that you know we're fine, and we can see you're hunky-dory…go home."

"What?"

Emily repeated herself. "Go home, Cor. You look exhausted. If I'm not mistaken, your man is foaming at the mouth to get you home and taken care of."

Corrie tilted her head up, as if she was actually looking at him. "But…can we go home?"

Quint kissed the top of her head, knowing what she meant. "Yeah, Dax and Hayden called in reinforcements. After the crime scene techs did their thing, they managed to get us an all new bed. I didn't want any reminders of what happened to Bethany there. It's all good, sweetheart."

"Promise?"

"Yes. I wouldn't bring you back there if I wasn't one-hundred percent sure it was safe and clean for you to go back to."

Corrie turned to her friends. "I love you guys. So much. I'll come back up and see you tomorrow."

"Okay. You know we love you too. Thank God you were smarter than those assholes."

Corrie smiled. "I don't know about smarter, but maybe more determined."

"Good enough."

"Come on, sweetheart. You're dead on your feet. Let's go home."

"Home. That sounds good."

Quint smiled huge. She was right. It did sound good.

He waited patiently as Corrie hugged Emily one more time, and leaned over Bethany and gave her an abbreviated hug and kiss on the cheek. She came back to him and reached for his hand. "Love you guys. See you tomorrow."

Quint led Corrie out of the room and down the hall to the waiting area. He gave a few chin lifts to the doctors and nurses who waved as they went by. He couldn't wait to get Corrie home.

CORRIE WAS RELIEVED to be back in Quint's house. They were standing in his bedroom. He'd dragged her to his room the second they'd arrived.

"You aren't afraid to be back here?"

Corrie shook her head. "No. One, you're here with me. And two, Isaac knocked me out as soon as I opened the door. I don't remember anything that happened. I'm guessing Bethany isn't going to want to come over for a very long time, but me? I'm good."

Quint hugged Corrie to him, loving how she snuggled up against him without hesitation. He had a lot he wanted to say to her, but wanted to get her clean and comfortable first. "Good. Go ahead and shower. I want nothing more than to hold you against me as soon as I can."

"You want to shower with me?" Corrie asked shyly.

Quint kissed her forehead. "If I get in that shower, I won't be able to take my hands off of you."

"And that's bad because…"

"Because I want to hold you. To reassure myself that you're really okay. I've had a shit day, I wasn't sure if I'd ever hold you warm and breathing in my arms again. I need you in my bed, in my arms."

"Okay, Quint. I'll be quick. I need that too."

"I love you, Corrie."

"I love you too."

"Shower, I'll be waiting in our bed."

Corrie nodded and Quint kissed her once more before turning her toward the bathroom.

He stripped down to his boxers and waited for Corrie to emerge from the shower, which had quickly filled with steam as she cleaned off the dirt from the events of the day.

Within ten minutes, Corrie padded out of the bathroom with only a towel wrapped around her body. Quint had never seen anything so beautiful in all his life. And she was all his.

"Come here, sweetheart."

Corrie walked cautiously to the bed with one arm out in front of her, making sure she didn't run into anything. When her knees hit the mattress, she held out her hand toward where Quint's voice had been coming from. Quint took it in his and watched as she unhooked the towel and it dropped to the floor.

"Holy shit, Corrie. You are so fucking beautiful."

She smiled. "Scoot over."

He did and she crawled under the sheets and into his arms.

"It doesn't smell like you anymore."

"What?"

"The sheets. They don't smell like you anymore. I hate that."

"They will soon. Don't worry." Quint felt his heart clench as Corrie nuzzled into him. She put her nose into his neck and inhaled deeply.

"But *you* smell like you, so it'll have to do," she teased.

Quint rolled Corrie under him. He put his legs on either side of hers, pushing his hips into hers, and rested his elbows next to her shoulders. He knew he was probably squishing her, but he needed to feel every part of her under every part of him.

"I know I told you this today, but I am so proud of you. I've seen a lot of brave things in my life. Battered women having the guts to leave abusive husbands, single parents raising handicapped kids by themselves, inner-city kids resisting the lure of gangs and drugs, firefighters rushing into burning buildings as everyone else rushes out."

Corrie took a breath to interrupt, but Quint hurried on.

"Even Mackenzie and Mickie, Dax and Cruz's women, continually impress the hell out of me. But when I was on my way to you, I have to tell you, I wasn't sure what I'd find. I thought you'd be scared and, I'm ashamed to admit…broken."

"Quint…"

Quint ignored her attempt to stop him again and forged ahead. "Hayden was the one who told me that

I was underestimating you. And she was right. She was so fucking right. You didn't need me to save you. You saved yourself. Blind, scared, hurting, and having no idea where the fuck you were…you still figured out a way to help yourself." He shook his head in amazement. "I'll never underestimate or doubt you again. You can do anything you want. And I love you for it."

"Can I talk now?" Corrie's voice was soft and serious.

Quint kissed the tip of her nose. "Yeah, you can talk."

"The only reason I was brave is because I knew you were on your way to me."

"Damn straight."

"Hey, it's my turn." Her hands rested on Quint's biceps, and she stroked the words inked on his arm unknowingly.

"Sorry, sweetheart. Continue."

"Thank you. As I said. The only reason I even tried to get away was to give you time to get to me. I know what he wanted to do to me. He took great pleasure in telling me how he was going to kill me and what he was going to do to me before he blew my brains out. But I wanted to live with every fiber of my being. For the first time in my life, I loved a man, and I wanted to experience that. I got mad. I didn't want them to take that from me. I wasn't brave, Quint. I was scared out of my mind every second I was out there."

"But you did it anyway."

Corrie nodded. "I did it anyway, because I knew you were on your way. If I could find a way to stay alive, you'd take care of Isaac and Dimitri."

"Of course. I'll always take care of you, sweetheart. All you ever have to do is wait, and whenever you need help, I'll be there."

"I know."

"When are we moving the rest of your stuff over here?"

"What?"

"The rest of your things. We need to talk to your landlord and put in your notice. You're moving in with me as soon as you can."

Corrie wanted to argue with him, but it was hard when there was nothing that would make her happier than living permanently with Quint. Knowing he was just as anxious for it was a heady feeling. "I'm already here. I have no desire to go anywhere."

Quint rested his forehead against hers. "I love you."

·"I love you."

When Quint didn't move, Corrie ran her hand

over the back of his head and leaned up to whisper where she thought his ear was. "Are you going to make love to me or what?"

Quint didn't budge an inch, but she felt him smile against her. "Yeah, I'm going to make love to you. Then I'm going to fuck you. Then eat you out, then fuck you again. That meet with your approval?"

"Oh yeah, as long as I can return the favor."

Quint eased off Corrie just long enough to push his boxers down and off, then he was back. "Lay back and let me show you how appreciative I am that you're a brave, badass woman. *My* brave, badass woman."

Corrie stretched her hands over her head and arched her back. "Have at it. I'm all yours."

EPILOGUE

"What I did is no more amazing than what you went through, Mackenzie," Corrie insisted. A couple of weeks had passed since Dimitri and Isaac had kidnapped her, and Quint had introduced her to Mackenzie and Mickie, Dax and Cruz's girlfriends. She'd gotten to know both men fairly well, since they'd made a point to come over to Quint's house to check on her when he was on shift and couldn't be home with her. Today they were all hanging out at a bar and reminiscing about the crappy things that happened to them, much to the chagrin of their men.

"That's not true. I can't believe you had the guts to wander outside of a house when you had no idea where you were and not only that, but you actually evaded tweedle-dee and tweedle-dum," Mackenzie enthused. "All I did was lie there and cry, hoping Dax would find me."

"You're both super women, all right?" Mickie said in exasperation.

Mackenzie turned to the other woman and teased, "You are the crazy one in the group though, Mickie. Getting all slutted up and marching into a motorcycle club as if you were the bionic woman or something. I swear I'll see you in that outfit I've heard so much about one of these days."

Mickie chuckled. "Yeah, not my finest moment for sure."

Corrie knew that Mickie's sister had been killed in the raid that had happened during the party Mickie had crashed. "I'm sorry about your sister, Mickie. Seriously."

"Thanks, Corrie. Me too. But looking back, I don't think she would've changed. I'm not saying I'm glad that she was killed, but I think her life would've continued to spiral downward if it didn't happen."

Because Corrie's hearing was so much better than everyone else's due to her blindness, she heard Cruz say to Mickie in a soft voice, trying to soothe her, "I love you, Mickie."

She turned to Quint before she heard Mickie's response, "Thank you for introducing me to your friends."

"You're welcome."

"I thought Penelope was going to be here tonight?" Corrie was intrigued with the petite firefighter. Quint had told her she was The Army Princess, the soldier who had been kidnapped while on a mission in Turkey. She remembered hearing the news stories about her, but hadn't realized Sledge was her brother, and the man behind all the intense media attention the case had gotten. It was almost unreal.

"She had planned on it, but she took a trip up to Fort Hood for something or other," Quint told her. "It's kinda crazy that this Tex character who TJ knows and who figured out where you had been taken, is the same person who helped coordinate her rescue, not once but twice." He shook his head, amazed at how things seemed to work out. "I'm sure you'll meet her soon. She's been dying to sit down with you too. She told me that if I was this head over heels in love, then you had to be amazing."

Corrie blushed. She didn't even know the woman, but she seemed like someone she'd get along with really well. Corrie leaned against Quint and listened to the conversation going on around her.

"Can you believe the calendar is actually going to happen?" Mackenzie asked her friend Laine, who had joined them at the bar.

"No. Actually I'm shocked you convinced your new boss to go ahead with it," Laine told her best friend, taking a drink.

"Calendar?" Corrie asked with a tilt of her head.

"Yeah, a charity thing. Every year my company does something to raise money for the community, and now that we have all these hotties at our beck and call, we decided a calendar was a great idea! This year we're going to do law enforcement, and hopefully next year we'll do the firefighter thing. Of course we don't have all of the models yet." Mack looked up at Dax with big doe eyes, then continued, "But we're working on it. Even Hayden has agreed to pose for us."

"So it's not just men?" Corrie queried.

"Nope...well, mostly. Most of the women don't want to have anything to do with being in it, but we convinced Hayden."

Hayden rolled her eyes at Mackenzie. "You didn't 'convince' me, Mack. You threatened and blackmailed me."

Everyone laughed.

"What's she holding over your head?"

"Mack, if you answer Corrie, you'll die," Hayden threatened.

Mackenzie held up her hands in capitulation. "My lips are sealed, but we *do* need at least one other guy. I'm pretty sure I've got all the others lined up."

"I might know someone," Daxton told Mack.

Her head whipped around so quickly it was comical. "Really? Who?"

"There's a guy at work. His name is Wes and he works with me."

"A Texas Ranger?" Corrie asked.

"Yeah. And a cowboy."

"I vote yes," Laine chimed in.

"You don't even know what he looks like!" Mack exclaimed.

"I bet he's hot. Is he hot, Dax?"

"I'm not sure about that. I'm not an expert of what's hot and what's not as far as you ladies go, but he *is* always getting hit on when we go to calls."

"Oh yeah, he's hot," Corrie said decisively. "Hayden? Do you know him? Is he hot?"

"On a scale of one to ten? I'd say he's at least a twelve," the law enforcement officer sighed in a breathy voice.

Everyone laughed.

"Great, it's a done deal. Daxton, get me his number and I'll somehow get him on board. Laine, you'll go with me for the shoot right? We can totally use the cowboy angle because none of the other guys are into that. Does he have a ranch? Yeah, I bet he does. Laine, we can go together and scope him out and see if he's got any hot ranch hands. We need more eye candy in our life. I need to get with the photographer and set everyone's sessions up, then talk to the printer and find out what the final schedule is going to be, and—"

Dax put his hand over Mack's mouth and held up his glass. "Since we're here to celebrate Corrie's awesomeness and climbing-a-tree-like-a-monkey ability, I would like to propose a toast...to Corrie. You are an amazing woman who doesn't let anything get her down. I admire your stubbornness and resilience. You are one tough chick and a perfect match for Quint. Welcome to our family."

Corrie couldn't see the men and women sitting around the table, but she knew they were all looking at her and Quint and smiling. She'd surprised herself in the forest, but she supposed the motivation to stay alive for Quint had been strong. She raised her glass and said in return, "I didn't do it myself. I knew Quint...and you guys...were on your way. That you'd find me. That's what let me keep going even when I was scared." She took a breath and turned to where she knew Laine, Hayden, TJ, Conor, and Calder were sitting.

"I hope you guys find the person out there who was made just for you. Don't give up, he or she is out there somewhere, and you'll never know when you'll meet them."

"Lord is this getting mushy," Hayden complained good naturedly.

"Thank you for being brave. For not letting those assholes get you down," Quint said and leaned over and kissed Corrie on the side of the head. "I love you. You mean the world to me."

Everyone sighed in contentment at witnessing the love between Quint and Corrie. She'd shown them all that just because a person had a disability, it didn't mean they were helpless.

After clinking glasses and drinking their toast, talk turned back to the calendar, and other work related incidents.

Corrie snuggled into Quint and let the conversation roll over her head. She was content to sit with her new friends, and boyfriend, and soak in the goodness that surrounded them all. Life was good, and she was very very lucky.

BE sure to check out the next book in the series...*Justice for Laine* . Available NOW!

JOIN my Newsletter and find out about sales, free

books, contests and new releases before anyone else!! Click HERE

Want to know when my books go on sale? Follow me on Bookbub HERE!

Would you like Susan's Book Protecting Caroline (SEAL of Protection series) for FREE?
Click HERE

Also by Susan Stoker

Badge of Honor: Texas Heroes Series

Justice for Mackenzie

Justice for Mickie

Justice for Corrie

Justice for Laine (novella)

Shelter for Elizabeth

Justice for Boone

Shelter for Adeline

Shelter for Sophie

Justice for Erin

Justice for Milena

Shelter for Blythe

Justice for Hope

Shelter for Quinn

Shelter for Koren

Shelter for Penelope

Delta Team Two Series

Shielding Gillian

Shielding Kinley (Aug 2020)

Shielding Aspen (Oct 2020)

Shielding Riley (Jan 2021)

Shielding Devyn (May 2021)

Shielding Ember (Sept 2021)

Shielding Sierra (TBA)

Delta Force Heroes Series

Rescuing Rayne

Rescuing Aimee (novella)

Rescuing Emily

Rescuing Harley

Marrying Emily (novella)

Rescuing Kassie

Rescuing Bryn

Rescuing Casey

Rescuing Sadie (novella)

Rescuing Wendy

Rescuing Mary

Rescuing Macie (novella)

SEAL of Protection: Legacy Series

Securing Caite

Securing Brenae (novella)

Securing Sidney

Securing Piper

Securing Zoey

Securing Avery (May 2020)

Securing Kalee (Sept 2020)

Securing Jane (novella) (Feb 2021)

SEAL Team Hawaii Series

Finding Elodie (Apr 2021)
Finding Lexie (Aug 2021)
Finding Kenna (Oct 2021)
Finding Monica (TBA)
Finding Carly (TBA)
Finding Ashlyn (TBA)

Ace Security Series

Claiming Grace
Claiming Alexis
Claiming Bailey
Claiming Felicity
Claiming Sarah

Mountain Mercenaries Series

Defending Allye
Defending Chloe
Defending Morgan
Defending Harlow
Defending Everly
Defending Zara
Defending Raven (June 2020)

Silverstone Series

Trusting Skylar (Dec 2020)
Trusting Taylor (Mar 2021)
Trusting Molly (July 2021)

Trusting Cassidy (Dec 2021

SEAL of Protection Series

Protecting Caroline

Protecting Alabama

Protecting Fiona

Marrying Caroline (novella)

Protecting Summer

Protecting Cheyenne

Protecting Jessyka

Protecting Julie (novella)

Protecting Melody

Protecting the Future

Protecting Kiera (novella)

Protecting Alabama's Kids (novella)

Protecting Dakota

Stand Alone

The Guardian Mist

Nature's Rift

A Princess for Cale

A Moment in Time- A Collection of Short Stories

Lambert's Lady

Special Operations Fan Fiction

http://www.AcesPress.com

Beyond Reality Series

Outback Hearts

Flaming Hearts

Frozen Hearts

Writing as Annie George:

Stepbrother Virgin (erotic novella)

ABOUT THE AUTHOR

New York Times, USA Today and *Wall Street Journal* Bestselling Author Susan Stoker has a heart as big as the state of Texas where she lives, but this all American girl has also spent the last fourteen years living in Missouri, California, Colorado, and Indiana. She's married to a retired Army man who now gets to follow *her* around the country.

She debuted her first series in 2014 and quickly followed that up with the SEAL of Protection Series, which solidified her love of writing and creating stories readers can get lost in.

If you enjoyed this book, or any book, please consider leaving a review. It's appreciated by authors more than you'll know.

www.stokeraces.com
susan@stokeraces.com